Miss Popularity
and the Best Friend Disaster

candy apple books... just for you.
sweet. Fresh. Fun. Take a bite!

The Accidental Cheerleader by Mimi McCoy

The Boy Next Door by Laura Dower

Miss Popularity by Francesco Sedita

How to Be a Girly Girl in Just Ten Days by Lisa Papademetriou

Drama Queen by Lara Bergen

The Babysitting Wars by Mimi McCoy

Totally Crushed by Eliza Willard

I've Got a Secret by Lara Bergen

Callie for President by Robin Wasserman

Making Waves by Randi Reisfeld and H. B. Gilmour

The Sister Switch by Jane B. Mason and Sarah Hines Stephens

Accidentally Fabulous by Lisa Papademetriou

Confessions of a Bitter Secret Santa by Lara Bergen

Accidentally Famous by Lisa Papademetriou

Star-Crossed by Mimi McCoy

Accidentally Fooled by Lisa Papademetriou

Miss Popularity Goes Camping by Francesco Sedita

Life, Starring Me! by Robin Wasserman

Juicy Gossip by Erin Downing

Accidentally Friends by Lisa Papademetriou

Snowfall Surprise by Jane B. Mason and Sarah Hines Stephens

The Sweetheart Deal by Holly Kowitt

Rumor Has It by Jane B. Mason and Sarah Hines Stephens

Super Sweet 13 by Helen Perelman

Wish You Were Here, Liza by Robin Wasserman

See You Soon, Samantha by Lara Bergen

Miss You, Mina by Denene Millner

Winner Takes All by Jenny Santana

Ice Dreams by Lisa Papademetriou

Miss Popularity
and the Best Friend Disaster

FRANCESCO SEDITA

SCHOLASTIC INC.

New York Toronto London Auckland
Sydney Mexico City New Delhi Hong Kong

No part of this publication may be reproduced, stored in a retrieval system, or transmitted in any form or by any means, electronic, mechanical, photocopying, recording, or otherwise, without written permission of the publisher. For information regarding permission, write to Scholastic Inc., Attention: Permissions Department, 557 Broadway, New York, NY 10012.

ISBN 978-0-545-16247-0

Copyright © 2011 by Francesco Sedita

All rights reserved. Published by Scholastic Inc. SCHOLASTIC, CANDY APPLE, and associated logos are trademarks and/or registered trademarks of Scholastic Inc.

Text design by Steve Scott
The text type was set in Bulmer.

12 11 10 9 8 7 6 5   13 14 15 16/0

Printed in the U.S.A.   40
First printing, April 2011

I'll show you what shoes to wear,

How to fix your hair—

Everything that really counts

To be popular.

—Glinda, *Wicked*

CHAPTER 1

Miss Twelve-Going-on-Fabulous

Cassie Cyan Knight looked at her green Swatch. 6:02! OMG, she had to get inside! Her nightly iChat with her best friend, Erin Donaldson, was about to begin. She'd been sitting on the lawn, relaxing with the newest J.Crew catalog, and had totally lost track of time. (And those periwinkle culottes on page 23 were a very good reason to get distracted. They were adorable!) Cassie jumped up and ran to the front door, her bare feet bouncing off the soft, warm grass, the golden Maine sun bright above.

It was May, at long last. Hooray! It had been six months since the Knight family had moved to Maine from Houston.

Six months since Cassie had been with any of her Texas girls, including Erin.

Six months of snowstorms, wearing boots almost all the time, and freezing cold temps.

Six months of camping and trees and nature.

Six months of being a student at Oak Grove, a private school that was *so* different from her beloved Sam Houston Middle School, back in big ol' Texas.

But now: The snow had finally lost the fight and warm, breezy days set the scene. Sandals were more than a fashion statement, they were a necessity. There was just one month of school left and, far more important, just eight days until Cassie's thirteenth birthday! She'd dreamed of this moment for years. She'd finally be a full-fledged teenager and one step closer to high school. Of course, it would be a bittersweet birthday without the Texas crew, but Cassie had made her peace with that.

*Life Rule #14: Sometimes,
what are you gonna do?*

She knew her girls were always with her in spirit. And she also knew that there were some super-exciting birthday plans for her in Maine.

After these six months, Cassie finally felt settled into her new life. She had to admit that she was becoming more and more an Oak Grovian and less a Sam Houston Spur.

Of course, there were lots of end-of-school things going on, too, like finals and papers and getting the yearbook out the door in time to print. Cassie's life felt so busy sometimes, she wondered how she'd ever do everything that adults were expected to do. But it's not worth stressing, she often reminded herself. She wasn't even thirteen yet. There had to be time for fun, too!

Cassie ran past the blueberry bushes and up the wooden front steps of her house, her red tresses flying behind her. This was the first spring in her life without the dreaded Texas humidity, so there was as much spring in her curls as there was in her step. She threw open the front door and bounded up the stairs to her bedroom.

"Cass!" her mother called from the dining room. "You have exactly twenty-seven minutes until supper!"

"Okay, Sheila!" Cassie hollered back. "Sheila" was so much more modern than plain old "Mom." Cassie also called her dad "Paul."

She ran into her bedroom, admiring, as she always did, the meticulously planned chocolate-brown and vanilla-white theme. Cassie missed so much about Texas, including her old house, which was much less creaky and creepy than their house in Maine. But Cassie's bedroom here was stellar. The browns and whites, with just a pop of color here and there. The teal phone. The red leather journal on her nightstand, that she never really wrote in because it was more for decoration than secrets. And the yellow shirt on Bob the Teddy Bear, who no longer lived hidden in the closet. He was now proudly featured on the center of her bed. He'd been through a lot with Cassie. He deserved to be comfortable.

Cassie was still in the process of choosing wall hangings, so her walls were bare, except for a few framed pics. There were the Texas girls, two years ago, all dressed as Powerpuffs at Erin's house one silly sleepover night. Laura Dean, the third in Cassie's Musketeers, won the unofficial Most Dedicated award, painting huge eyes on her face to look as Powerpuff-like as possible. There was a photo of Sheila and Paul back in April, at the Oak

4

Grove Fash Bash, which had raised a ton of money for tree planting. And, of course, there was a photo of Cassie at her very first—and very interesting—camping trip with Etoile Davey, her bestest Maine friend, and Mary Ellen McGinty, her Maine frenemy. The three girls stood grinning triumphantly after bungee jumping.

Sitting in the edge of that frame was another picture. One that Cassie was hesitant to hang on its own. It was taken right after the relay race on the same camping trip. Etoile was grinning ear to ear with her crush, Seth Gordon. Cassie stood next to them, with Jonah Freeman, Etoile's best guy friend since birth. And Cassie's . . . crush?! Just thinking it made her woozy with confusion. But maybe. She wasn't sure yet. Lately, her heart went all haywire when he was around. Ever since she'd seen him sing "Don't Stop Believin'" during nano-oke, he just seemed sort of . . . cute? He was crush material, for sure. He'd always been nice to Cassie, helping with the Fash Bash and pre-al, and being funny and understanding of her fear of all things camping. But he was practically Etoile's brother!

So Cassie hadn't told Etoile about her maybe-crush. She didn't know how Etoile would take the news. Cassie had to be certain of her feelings before she had that difficult conversation.

Cassie ran to her desk, where Erin waited on her glossy iMac screen. iChatting was their daily check-in and Cassie adored it. Time to catch up. Time to gossip a little. Compare homework and ask for help. Cassie loved to hear what was going on back in Houston, although Erin always said nothing was new in Houston. But it was all new to Cassie!

She plunked down at her desk and clicked ACCEPT on the iChat window.

Erin's picture zoomed large and filled Cassie's screen. Even though a long school day had just ended, Erin was still completely fresh looking. Her lip gloss, a pinker tone than usual, sparkled through the monitor. Her blond curls, bigger than ever these days, were piled high on her head. Cassie felt a pang of homesickness. *No one does big hair better than Texas,* she thought. Since the move to Maine, Cassie's curls had gotten tamer. She even straightened sometimes!

"Sisterfriend!" Cassie yelled, laughing. She'd

heard Oprah call someone that once and thought it was hysterical.

"Sisterfriend!" Erin yelled back. Just then, her little labradoodle started barking and spinning in the background.

"Snoodle!" Cassie yelled. The silly dog stopped his tantrum and cocked his head, looking directly into Erin's computer, at Cassie. "Hi, baby!" Cassie shouted all the way from Maine.

"How was your day?" Erin asked.

Just then another IM window popped up on Cassie's screen. It was Jonah!

"Cass, do you need to get that?" Erin asked.

Cassie's face flushed. "Uh, wait one sec."

She clicked on to Jonah's IM.

JONAHROCKS: Earth to Cassie Knight. Paging Cassie Knight.
MISSCASS: Hey!
JONAHROCKS: What's up?
MISSCASS: Nothing much. Just chatting with Erin in Houston.
JONAHROCKS: That's cool.

Cassie's heart pounded.

JONAHROCKS: Just wanted to say hi . . . So, hi.

MISSCASS: Hi!

JONAHROCKS: Talk to you later?

MISSCASS: Sure! ☺

Cassie turned back to her camera.

"WHO was that?" Erin asked.

"Oh, no one!" Cassie said, trying to be nonchalant, but almost yelling.

"Uh-uh."

Cassie couldn't get anything by Erin.

"Okay, it was Jonah."

"Etoile's friend?"

"My friend."

"OMG! He looks really cute in those pics you sent," Erin exclaimed, smiling.

Cassie wanted—needed—to change the subject quickly. "Okay, so I was asking about your day. How was it?"

"No, I was asking about *your* day," Erin pointed out. "But since you're asking, my day was good. Really good, actually." She began fidgeting. Erin only fidgeted when she was nervous.

"Wait, what's up with you?" Cassie asked.

"I have some news . . ." Erin said, leaning in close to the camera.

"What?!" Cassie asked excitedly.

"Well, I know that your birthday is coming up, Miss Twelve-Going-on-Fabulous!"

Cassie laughed. "Yes," she said with an exaggerated hair flip. "I *am* pretty fab."

"And, I just thought that you should have a little piece of Texas there to celebrate with you," Erin went on calmly.

"Okay?" Cassie said.

"So, after much thinking and deliberation with Laura . . ."

Cassie couldn't imagine what the surprise was going to be. New cowboy boots? Her fave cupcakes from Sugarbabe's? Something fringe-tastic?

Erin continued, "We decided that . . ."

"Oh my G! What? You're killing me!" Cassie leaned so close to the camera, she was sure Erin could only see her eyebrows.

Erin's serious face cracked into a huge ear-to-ear grin. "We're coming to visit!"

"WHAT?!" Cassie gasped.

Erin's words spilled out in a rush. "Laura's dad

has to go to Maine for business, and she asked if he would take us so we could celebrate your b-day, and he said YES!"

"Wait, where in Maine?" Cassie asked. Maine was small compared to Texas, but not *that* small.

"Portland!"

"Portland is, like, ten minutes away!" Cassie couldn't believe her luck.

"I know!" Erin yelled, Snoodle barking louder now.

"When?" Cassie asked, clicking onto her iCal.

"Um, just one day before your birthday! May twentieth!" Erin said, doing the same.

Just one week away! Cassie jumped out of her chair and spun around. "This is the best news EVER!" she squealed. "Wait, what about school?"

"We have Friday and Monday off for parent/teacher conferences," Erin explained. She followed Cassie's lead and jumped up, spinning. The poor, confused dog did the same.

Cassie regained her composure and sat back down. "Okay, I am so excited! You are the bestest best friend in the galaxy!"

"So are you! That's why we're coming!"

Cassie thought about the weekend for a moment. "Now, wait a minute, there are *so many* good things happening. Next Friday, after school, Etoile and I are getting mani-pedis and shopping and eating French fries and ice-cream sundaes for dinner at the mall. That's the start of my birthday celebration."

Erin was quiet for a second and then said, "Oh, so, is it weird if me and Laura are going to be there, too? I didn't really even think about it."

"Weird?! Are you crazy? Of course not. It's all my favorite people in one place! It's perfect!" She smiled at Erin. "And then, we'll do some sight-seeing on Saturday and get ready for my roller-skating party!"

Cassie had already told Erin all about the party. Back in Texas, they had always gone roller-skating together. It felt so 1980s cool, and Cassie loved skating on four wheels. She never did well with Rollerblading. But she felt great on skates. And she hadn't been on hers in far too long. She was planning one of the best parties *ever*. And now, it would only be better with Erin and Laura on the guest list!

"Okay, wait a sec," Erin said. She ran to her closet, pulled the door open, and started to flip through the hangers. "I need you to help me figure out what I'm going to wear," she called over her shoulder.

"FASHION SHOW!" Cassie yelled.

As Erin ran back and forth from her closet, flashing fashions to the camera, Cassie laughed with sheer joy. She'd been dreaming of her thirteenth birthday since she was nine. And now her special day would include her best friends on the planet, awesome music, and her very pink roller skates.

CHAPTER 2

Friends Becoming Friends

The next morning, Cassie couldn't wait to see Etoile in school. The girls hadn't spoken since last period the day before, because Etoile's parents had taken her to Portland to see the big production of *Wicked*. They'd texted while they were getting ready for school but Cassie wanted to share the big news in person.

Cassie sat in Mrs. O'Leary's pre-al class, doing her best to concentrate. The final exam was coming up fast and Cassie was struggling with the prep work. And based on her last quiz grade—a big, fat 78—Cassie had some concentrating to do. But that 78 had been beyond her control:

There was a very important *So You Think You Can Dance* on the night before and integers just weren't as appealing. Cassie felt bad; she liked Mrs. O'Leary, who tried hard to make math easy and fun. But somehow it just didn't work for Cassie.

Even though she had no morning classes with Etoile, she had pre-al with Jonah and Seth. Since the camping trip, Cassie, Etoile, Jonah, and Seth had become a sort of foursome. Seth was the sweetest guy, and superdoop cute. (Though *maybe* not as cute as Jonah.) Now, sitting next to the boys in class, she wanted to tell them all about the Texas girls' trip. Instead, she had to focus on the linear equations review.

But as her mind meandered, Cassie began making a list of things she wanted to do when the girls arrived. A long weekend wasn't going to be long enough, Cassie was certain.

To do with Erin and Laura:
* *Meet Etoile!*
* *And everyone else, including Mr. B and PV!!*
* *Oak Grove tour*
* *Ooooh, new house and new bedroom tour*

14

* Sightseeing: The mall, the performing arts high school, the little pond near Etoile's house
* Eating: Blueberries! And burgers from Sullivan's!!

At that moment, the bell rang. Cassie flipped her green notebook closed and gathered her stuff up manically.

"What's the rush?" Jonah asked.

Cassie giggled, knowing she must have looked a little strange. "I haven't spoken to Etoile since yesterday."

"Lucky you," Jonah joked.

"Very funny. We have study hall together next and I have a lot to fill her in on."

"I bet," Jonah said, rolling his eyes in his too-cool way.

"Oh, please, you know you'd be sitting with us if you were there!"

"She's right, Freeman. You know it," Seth said.

"Thank you, Seth," Cassie said smugly. She grabbed her Deery-Lou tote bag. "Okay, see you later!"

Jonah called after her. "You need help with pre-al tonight?"

"Of course I do!" Cassie said, almost blushing. And with that, she was off to study hall and, finally, Etoile.

When Cassie walked into Mr. B's study hall, Etoile was sitting at her desk, her head buried in a text-book. Cassie wondered how Etoile would do over the summer, without school.

Cassie plunked down. "Hello, Starshine! How was the show?"

Etoile pulled her head out of the book. She looked exhausted. Her brown eyes were droopy, and her shiny, chestnut locks seemed unin-spired. She must have gotten back late from *Wicked*.

"Starshine is a little tired," Etoile replied, her voice deeper than normal.

"Tell me everything," Cassie said. She abso-lutely loved musicals. For her tenth birthday, she and Sheila and Paul saw *Mamma Mia!* in Houston. Cassie lived for it. The bright lights, the shimmer-ing costumes, the dancing in the aisles.

"Cass, it was brilliant!" Etoile's face lit up. "She actually flies! It's the best thing ever." Etoile pulled her backpack onto her lap and dug through it wildly. "Here," she said, pulling out a CD of the sound track and handing it to Cassie. "I thought you'd like this."

"Thank you so much!" Cassie said, elated. She threw her arms around Etoile and pulled her in for a big squinch. Cassie really wanted to see the show.

Mary Ellen McGinty walked into the room then, a huge stack of books in her arms, her hair in a messy ponytail. Cassie would have done anything to get Mary Ellen's hair out of that ratty old elastic but she was taking baby steps.

The two very different girls had a rough start when Cassie arrived. It wasn't until the camping trip that they'd really bonded.

Mary Ellen put her books down on her desk and said good morning to a few people. She had respect at Oak Grove and was one of the super-smartest people in the school. She looked over at Etoile and Cassie.

"Hello, ladies," she said, as chipper as possible. She then noticed that Cassie was holding the *Wicked* CD. "I love that show!" she said loudly. Mary Ellen ran to Cassie's desk and pulled the CD out of her hands. "'Defying Gravity' is the best!"

Etoile and Cassie glanced at each other, startled by Mary Ellen's enthusiasm.

"Etoile saw it last night," Cassie said.

"Oh, that's so great. I saw it with my folks when we went to New York last year." Cassie could practically see the stage lights glimmering in Mary Ellen's eyes.

Cassie didn't want to change the subject but she absolutely had to before the bell rang and Mr. B came in.

"I have news," Cassie began, beaming.

Mary Ellen and Etoile stopped talking and looked at Cassie. Mary Ellen put her finger up to say "one sec" and called Lynn Bauman, *her* best friend, over to hear. Lynn rushed over and crouched by Cassie's desk.

"Okay, ready?" Cassie asked.

"Ready!" Etoile answered enthusiastically.

"I am getting a queen-size gift from Texas for my birthday next week."

"A replica of the Alamo?" Etoile asked.

"A fringed, suede skirt?" Lynn chimed in.

"An even bigger bottle of hair spray?" Mary Ellen asked a little mockingly.

"Ha-ha," Cassie said. "And y'all are wrong! Although a suede skirt with just the right amount of fringe would be so cute for fall!" It had been a while since Cassie said "y'all." It felt good.

"Whatever," Mary Ellen said, rolling her eyes.

"And, besides, a big can of hair spray is so six months ago, Mary Ellen. I'm all natural spray now, if you didn't know." Cassie plumped her curls.

Mary Ellen chuckled.

"Cass!" Etoile said. "The suspense is killing us!"

"Okay, okay. My best friends from Texas—Erin and Laura—are coming to visit!"

"No WAY!" Etoile said.

"I know! I'm so excited for you to meet them." Cassie and Etoile fell into a spontaneous hug.

"That's so awesome. What a special birthday it's going to be," Lynn said, sweet as always.

"I forgot that you'd never met the Texas girls," Mary Ellen said to Etoile, her eyebrow arched.

"Just on iChat and stuff," Etoile said, smoothing

her hair. Cassie noticed that immediately. Etoile only smoothed her hair back when she was uncomfortable.

"It's going to be may-jah!" Cassie said in her best Victoria Beckham accent.

Mr. Blackwell came running in just as the bell rang. "Hi, everyone," he said out of breath. He'd started to ride his bike to school each morning since they'd returned from the camping trip. And since then, he was always a little late. But he was going green, and Cassie thought that was really cool.

Mr. B started giving some school updates. And even though she knew it was incredibly rude, Cassie had to give Etoile more details about the impending visit. She opened her notebook and wrote:

It's going to be so great!!! You guys are my favorite people and we're going to have a blast! ☺

Cassie truly hoped Etoile would be okay with Erin and Laura joining their BFF birthday celebration.

She slowly tugged the paper out of her notebook and slid it to Etoile. Though Etoile was übercool and chic, she was a total Nervous Nellie when it came to even remotely breaking a rule. Cassie softly cleared her throat. Nothing.

The moment Mr. B turned to face the whiteboard, she whispered, "E!"

Etoile looked over. Her eyes were heavy, like she was about to fall asleep at any moment. Cassie pointed down to the note. Etoile bugged her eyes out, which was secret-friend code for "You know I hate stuff like this."

But as she read the note, her tired eyes became happy. A tiny "awww" came out of her mouth.

Mr. B—and the entire classroom, for that matter—heard it. "Is there something you need, ladies?" their teacher asked.

"I'm sorry. No, we're good," Cassie said, feeling bad about interrupting.

Mr. Blackwell smiled. "That's okay." He turned around and continued to write something on the whiteboard.

Etoile wrote back to Cassie.

I can't wait to meet them.

So it's okay if they crash our night out??

OF COURSE!

Cassie grinned. There would be nothing to worry about. The birthday weekend looked perfect.

CHAPTER 3

Texas Special Delivery

If Cassie ever really needed a personal assistant or a fashion intern, this was the time. Between getting ready for finals, the birthday bash, and the Texas arrivals—not to mention all the Yearbook activities—the week flew by. Before she could blink, the day of her Texas Special Delivery was here.

And she still had no idea what to wear.

It would be a special moment: their first face-to-face, live, and in-person catch-up in six months. Six months! Cassie just couldn't believe it. It called for a special outfit.

Life Rule #49: Special MEANS special!

She'd torn out some outfits from *Teen Vogue* and pinned them on her inspiration board, right next to a picture of the awesomely elegant Natalie Portman. Cassie was still a Texas girl, of course, but she also had a new Maine style that she was proud to rock. Finding the perfect balance would be a testament to her fashion abilities.

Etoile sat on Cassie's bed, reading a magazine, while Cassie flitted around the room, trying to settle on an outfit. Cassie had gotten a text from Erin when they landed about an hour ago. The plan was for Cassie to meet the girls at their hotel in Portland, and get their own table at the hotel restaurant. Meanwhile, Paul and Laura's dad would sit together and catch up.

"So, what do you think about this?" Cassie asked Etoile, holding up her wrist to show a white, plastic, beaded bracelet.

Etoile glanced up from the article she was reading. "I love that bracelet, you know that," she said, smiling. "I think I've borrowed it, like, six times."

"So, I should wear it?" Cassie asked, looking at the bracelet in the mirror. Did it clash with her green pleated tennis skirt (which was an Etoile original, on loan) or were the styles too different to combine?

"Sure." Etoile went back to reading the magazine.

Over the past few days, Cassie noticed that Etoile had been quieter than usual. Plus, whenever Cassie brought up the Texas girls' visit, Etoile seemed to change the subject. But Cassie wasn't sure if she was imagining it or not.

Cassie focused on her hair in the full-length. She'd straightened it before school that morning and now regretted it. She didn't want to look too different when she saw Erin and Laura. She still wanted to look like Cassie for them.

"I shouldn't have straightened my hair this morning," Cassie said, defeated.

"Why?" Etoile asked, without looking up from the magazine.

"Because. Curly hair was my thing in Houston."

"But you're not in Houston anymore," Etoile said with a shrug.

"I know. I just . . ." Cassie shrugged, too. "I want to look like me."

"You do look like you. Who else could you look like?" Etoile asked.

"I don't know," Cassie said, examining her hair in the mirror.

Etoile rolled her eyes and went back to her magazine.

"E?" Cassie said, even more confused than before. "Why are you being weird?"

Etoile looked up. "Me? I'm not being weird."

"Okay. I think you are. But maybe I'm wrong," Cassie said, busying herself with the clasp on her gold "Cassie" necklace. That was one thing she would never stop wearing, no matter how long she lived in Maine.

The room was silent then. "Do you want to listen to music?" Cassie asked.

"Whatever you want," Etoile said without looking up again.

"E!" Cassie exclaimed. "What's up?" It *wasn't* her imagination this time.

Etoile sighed. She closed her eyes for a second, a telltale sign that she was about to spill some serious beanage.

"I'm really sorry," she said at last. "I think I'm just scared to meet Erin and Laura. I mean, what if they don't like me?" She smoothed her brown hair nervously.

"What?!" Cassie asked, sitting on the edge of her bed. "They are totally going to adore you."

Etoile sighed again. "They're not going to adore me just because you do. They could wind up hating me!" Etoile's head sank down.

Cassie reached out to squeeze her friend's hand. "Please! E. Listen. First of all, I wouldn't let them hate you. And second of all—this should have been first, actually—um, you're the best!"

Etoile lifted her head, half smiling. Cassie smiled back, so sincere, she was sure her heart would burst.

"Okay," Etoile said unconvincingly.

"Now." Cassie turned to face her. "Does this outfit get the stamp of approval?"

Etoile looked at her, studying everything with her steady eye. "Absolutely. You look great."

Cassie gave Etoile a big hug. They started flipping through the magazine together until Paul called from downstairs that it was time to go.

Cassie sat in the passenger seat of Paul's car, butterflies flying hard and fast in her stomach. Why was she nervous? She really liked the outfit she and Etoile had put together—the tennis skirt, a white polo shirt, green and white knee-high argyles, and her new Mary Janes. And the white plastic bracelet for a touch of flair. It was totally fun but also Maine and sporty.

Her straight hair still felt like a mistake. In Texas, curls defined Cassie. They were perfect for the Texas humidity. But now, in Maine, she could experiment with a lot of different styles. And ever since Etoile first flat-ironed her hair, Cassie had fallen in love. But now, tonight, it felt all wrong.

"How you doin', hon?" Paul asked.

"I'm good." Cassie sat for a moment, quiet. Paul always knew when something was up. "Why?" she asked, hoping he'd pull it out of her.

"Well, you're not changing the radio station every two seconds and you're not texting. And you're not talking. As far as car rides go, this is like the Twilight Zone." He turned to her and winked.

"Well . . ."

"Yes?" Paul said, his voice shifting into advice mode.

"I'm ridiculously nervous," Cassie said, feeling almost foolish.

28

"About seeing those guys after so long?" Paul asked, zeroing in on the problem right away. As always.

"Yes! And what if they don't like me anymore? Or Etoile? Or what if they've changed?" Cassie stopped at three questions. That was plenty.

"Okay. All good questions," Paul said. "Question One. What if they don't like you, huh?"

Cassie nodded enthusiastically, her straightened hair tickling her neck.

"Ridiculous and impossible. I won't even go on about this one. You talk and text with the Texas crew, what, fourteen times a day?"

Cassie giggled.

"And," Paul continued, "Erin and Laura are like your sisters."

He was right. Cassie took a deep breath.

"Question Two. Etoile. She's a big part of your life, Cass. And she's a great girl."

Cassie drew another deep breath. Again, he was right.

Paul turned on his blinker as they pulled into the hotel parking lot.

"As far as changing goes," Paul said, scratching his head. "Life is all about changes. Big and

29

small. Good and bad. You've changed. So have they, I bet."

Cassie nodded. Paul made good arguments.

"And so what?" he went on. "I bet most of the changes y'all have made are for the best. And you'll love each other even more."

Cassie took a final deep breath, the last of the butterflies disappearing with it. Paul was the best dad ever.

"Thanks, Dad," she said. Sometimes "Dad" was called for.

"Anytime," he said, pulling into a parking space. He put the car in PARK and looked over at Cassie. "And what about me? You haven't asked if I'm nervous to see Laura's dad after all this time."

Cassie couldn't believe how selfish she was! Of course she should have asked that question. "Oh, wow. I didn't even think about that. Are you really nervous?" she asked.

"Well, it has been a little while since I've seen Ed," he said, his voice trembling. Then he started to laugh. "No, I'm not nervous. I'm just pulling your leg, honey!"

Cassie burst out laughing, and gave him a fake punch on his arm. "Dad!"

"So, are we ready?" he asked, still laughing.

Cassie pulled down the visor above her and did some last-minute primping. Lips were glossed, lashes quickly separated. Hair was still problematic, but she wasn't going to focus on that now. "We are so ready!" she said.

They stepped out of the car and she grabbed Paul's hand. Together, they walked into the lobby, excited.

CHAPTER 4

Reunited!

Cassie couldn't get over how beautiful the hotel was. Everywhere she looked, wood shined back at her—the dark walls, the heavy upholstered furniture. An enormous old chandelier hung above her, and the long wooden floorboards squeaked as people walked. She'd never seen anything quite like it before and was certain that Erin and Laura hadn't either. She hoped they liked it.

While Cassie got cozy on a big, overstuffed couch, Paul went to the front desk to call up to the room. Near the couch there was a plaque that said the hotel had been there since 1837. Cassie felt a sense of history in Maine that she hadn't really felt in Texas, besides the story of the Alamo, of course. Maine was different. The air smelled salty, and the sunlight was more yellow, different from the white light of Houston. The roads curved through fields and fields of grass and wildflowers. So different, so lovely. Cassie took a deep breath and soaked in the perfection of the moment.

She pulled her phone out to text Erin and Laura.

We R here!!!

In a moment, Cassie got a message back from Erin:

YAY!!! xo

Just then, she heard the old, bronze elevator ding. She looked up and there they were. Erin and Laura. Her long-lost BFFs!!

Cassie shot out of her seat on the couch, past the front desk, and straight toward them. But both Erin and Laura looked right past Cassie.

"Um, hello?!" Cassie said.

Cassie watched as Erin's expression went from confusion to recognition.

"OMG!" she exclaimed. "Cass? Is it *you*?"

"What do you mean?" Cassie asked, shocked.

"Your hair!" Erin said. "It's so different!"

"And your outfit!" Laura said, her twang thick.

"Well, it's me!" Cassie laughed, throwing her arms open.

The three girls embraced, squealing and screaming so loud that some people turned to see what all the commotion was.

"Let me see *your* hair!" Cassie said, stepping back for a moment to examine Erin's big, blond curls. They were so enormous, Cassie wondered if Erin used soup cans as her rollers. "Our iChats have not done these babies justice!"

"Well," Erin said, "someone had to take over in the curl department!"

"You've certainly succeeded!" Cassie replied, giggling. Cassie gave her another big hug. As she did, she noticed the back of Erin's pink satin dress had a huge multicolored dragon on it. It was a pretty dragon. But Cassie couldn't believe it lived on a dress!

Cassie turned to Laura then. She wore a shimmery red shirt and dark jeans with butterflies embroidered on them. Her brown hair was piled up on top of her head in an over-sprayed twist. And a rhinestone butterfly was perched right at the center of her head. Cassie certainly had worn some crazy stuff in her day but Laura was really setting new standards. It felt almost foreign to Cassie, but she loved it.

"You are looking divine!" Cassie said to Laura. "This color is perfect on you!"

"Thanks!" Laura said. "I wanted to wear teal but didn't know if you were still against it!"

Cassie smiled. Teal used to be her favorite color but now she'd pretty much moved on. "I'm not against it! I just like green more these days!"

"Attention," Erin interrupted loudly, "Ms. Knight has moved on to a new color. Please alert the fashion media!"

Cassie felt her cheeks flush. Was Erin making fun of her?

"All right, girls," Paul said, "now that the screams are over, shall we have some dinner?"

Laura's dad laughed. He gave Cassie a big, Texas-size hug. "Cass! Look at you! You're growin' up, darlin'!"

"It's so great to see you!" Cassie responded.

"Seems like there's a lot for y'all to catch up

on," he said, his accent thicker than Cassie's favorite platform heels.

"I'll say," Paul said, smiling.

They were seated immediately in the hotel restaurant, and Cassie had to control herself from jumping up and down every two minutes. They ordered their food, then began talking as they sipped from their Shirley Temples, like they used to drink together when they were little girls.

"It's so, like, old-fashioned here," Laura said. She looked around, craning her head up and down, and from side to side. "It's so old and little and cute." Cassie knew exactly what Laura meant. So much of Maine was sweet and quaint, which surprised Cassie when she'd first arrived. But that sweetness quickly became one of her favorite things about her new home state.

"It seems kind of . . . empty everywhere," Erin said. "Like we're in the wilderness or something. I think it would freak me out if I lived here."

Cassie laughed. "No, it wouldn't. You'd get used to it."

"I just feel like there are wild animals and stuff everywhere!" Erin said.

Since her camping trip, Cassie knew all about those wild animals. But she also knew how cool it was to live near them. "Well, I've seen raccoons and deer and stuff. But Portland's a big city. I mean, it's not like we're in the middle of the woods!" she said, almost feeling defensive.

"We might as well be," Laura said, swatting at a bug Cassie didn't see.

It was time to change the subject, immediately. "Tell me how everything is in Houston," Cassie said.

"Okay, but before we do, I have to ask a question," Erin said. "What's up with the skirt you're wearing? I love it."

This made Cassie happy. She'd hoped they would notice. "It's an Etoile original," she said, popping out of her chair and showing them. "Look at these pleats! She did all of this." She ran her hand over the skirt to show the detailed work.

"Wow, she made that?" Laura asked.

"Well, she found it at a vintage store. And then she made it better." Cassie knew the word *vintage* would get a negative reaction but she was proud of Etoile and all her work.

"A vintage store?" Erin echoed, crinkling her

nose. Erin and Cassie always disagreed on the value of vintage. Cassie thought it was fabulous to rediscover. Erin thought it was a way to get cooties.

"Now I don't love it quite as much," Erin said, frowning in disapproval.

"Me neither!" Laura said, eying the skirt as if it was radioactive.

"Oh, c'mon!" Cassie said, more forcefully than she meant. "Vintage is where Etoile begins most of her fashions."

She sat down again. A strange moment passed by slowly, as they sipped their syrupy drinks. Was Cassie being supersensitive about Etoile? She hadn't meant to be.

Life Rule #61: Awkward silences are the worst. Avoid at all costs.

"Okay, give me the Houston dish!" Cassie said brightly.

Erin and Laura didn't miss a beat and brought Cassie up to speed on all of the happenings, including their pal Jen's movie date with a new boy who'd transferred into Sam Houston Middle School. Cassie couldn't believe there was a new classmate in her old school. Things really were changing.

They told her stories of the cafeteria; of the new gym teacher that had them working harder than ever and sweating more than ever, which was not so good for the boy-stink factor throughout the rest of the day; and about the new carpet in the library that smelled like chemicals so much that it made Annie Conrad pass out during study hall.

Cassie truly missed Houston but now, hearing her BTF (Best Texas Friends) tell her stories, it felt okay to not live there, for the first time ever. Life in Maine proved to be better and better each day. In Maine, Cassie discovered happiness in things she never even knew about in Texas: big, starry night skies, blueberries, and cool breezes.

Once the food arrived, Cassie was feeling more relaxed. It took a little bit of time for the girls to find their groove, but once they did, it was as if no time had passed at all. Cassie told the girls about things at Oak Grove, although they knew most of it, anyway, from their calls and chats. She even talked a little bit about Jonah.

"Do you think he'll ask you out on a date?" Laura asked, smiling.

"I have no idea! But I still don't want to say anything about it to Etoile. You have to promise to not say a word about this in front of her. I'll tell her soon. I'm just not ready yet."

"Totally," Erin said.

Cassie shot Laura a suspicious look. "And you?" she asked. Laura was terrible at keeping secrets.

"Promise!" Laura said.

As they shared two desserts, they went over their plans for the weekend.

"Okay," Cassie said. "Tomorrow, you guys are coming to Oak Grove at four o'clock. Etoile and I have Yearbook until then. When you get there, we'll show you around and then we'll head to my house and get ready for the mall."

"I can't wait to see your new school!" Laura said.

"Me neither!" Erin said. "Wait till you see our Grove outfits!"

Cassie felt a wave of nervousness wriggle through her, a flashback of her satin teal first-day dress. But that wasn't fair. Her Texas girls were her besties, inside and out.

Too soon, Paul and Laura's dad came over to tell the girls that it was time to go. Cassie gave Erin and Laura big hugs.

"Happy early birthday!" the girls both yelled.

Another hug.

And then before she knew it, Cassie was back in Paul's car, the windows misty from the salty Maine air, headed home.

CHAPTER 5

Happy Birthday, Dear Cassie!

Cassie's eyes popped open at 6:30 A.M. She had fifteen minutes more of sleep before her dreaded alarm blared. And although she adored her beauty sleep, she just couldn't wait to start her day.

Her thirteenth birthday!

Life Rule #13: Your thirteenth birthday is going to be the best birthday ever!

Sure, she'd written that on her eleventh birthday. And her twelfth. But Cassie knew thirteen would be a great one. She jumped out of bed, threw on her new zebra-print robe, and slid on her marabou slippers. She walked to the window, hoping that when she pulled back the curtains, she'd be greeted with Maine sunshine.

And she was! The sun shone down on the towering trees in the front yard, their deep, green leaves all dewy and thick. Cassie smiled and stretched her arms high above her head.

Just then, her phone buzzed. Cassie couldn't imagine who it could be so early. She snapped the phone open.

13 and Sassy! Love ya, Cassie.
xxEtoile

Cassie smiled and texted back:

U R the 1st! Thanks! CU SOON xo

As she walked out of her bedroom, her phone buzzed in her hand. Another text. This time, it was Jonah!

Happy Birthday! Hope the day is gr8! C U L8R. ☺

Cassie's jaw dropped. She hopped around in a little circle. Once she regained her cool, she wrote back.

Aw, sweet! Thanks!

She stared at the phone. Was that the right thing to say? Maybe it sounded too excited? Or too silly? She wished she could ask Etoile for advice.

"Cass!" Paul called from downstairs. "Get down here and let us begin the birthday celebration!!"

She had no choice. She hit SEND.

Excitedly, she ran down the stairs, clicking her fingernails against the banister as she did so. She was happy to be getting a mani tonight because there was an atrocious chip to deal with.

Life Rule #60: No chips. Ever.

She turned into the kitchen. Sheila and Paul sat at the kitchen table, reading the newspaper. There was a long box placed between them, wrapped in green paper with a bow on top. Cassie knew it had to be her gift.

"Good morning, sweetie!" Sheila exclaimed, setting her coffee cup down. She stood up and gave Cassie a big birthday hug. "Happy birthday!" she said. Cassie smiled. A hug from Sheila was always great.

Paul was right behind Sheila. A big hug and a kiss on the forehead. Cassie sat down at the table, and Sheila walked to the stove.

"Okay," she said. "Birthday girl's choice. Or I can surprise you."

There was nothing to consider for Cassie. "Surprise me, please!"

Sheila went to work, cracking eggs and whisking things. "So, Dad said the dinner with the girls was fun. Tell me about it!"

"I had an awesome time. I thought maybe things would be weird or something but they weren't. Not totally, anyway."

Paul looked up from the paper. "Not totally?"

"Well, I guess it's just a little weird to have them here after all this time. You know? They didn't even recognize me at first." Cassie still couldn't believe that.

Sheila looked at Cassie thoughtfully. "Really? It must have been your hair. You know, it's normal for a reunion like this to feel a little strained at first."

"Maybe," Cassie replied.

Sheila walked over to the table with the butter dish and real maple syrup, something Cassie never knew about until they moved to Maine. When her hands were free, she picked up the gift-wrapped box and handed it to Cassie.

"Happy thirteenth birthday, sweetheart," she said. "From me and Dad."

Paul folded up the paper quickly and stuck it under his chair. He sat up, at attention.

"Wow!" Cassie examined the bright, shiny green paper and the hand-tied teal bow. Last year, her entire gift was teal. It's funny how things change. "May I open it now?"

"Of course!" Sheila said.

Cassie opened the card first.

Life Rule #81: The real gift is the card, not what's in the box!

On the front of the card, there was the cutest picture of a pug puppy, wearing a birthday party hat. Inside, it read:

Dear Cass,

Thirteen is a big step. And you are definitely someone who knows how to handle life's big steps. We love you very much. And we're so proud of you. Thanks for being you.

Love,
Mom and Dad
(aka, Sheila and Paul!)

Cassie eyes filled with tears. "Thank you so much," she said softly. Sheila put her hand on Cassie's.

"Okay, open it! Open it!" Paul said. Cassie laughed at his goofiness. He was the worst when it came to opening presents.

She tore the paper carefully to reveal a smooth black box. Inside, sitting in a bed of shiny black satin, Cassie saw the most beautiful silver link bracelet. She tenderly picked it up. A tiny charm hung from the center link. A dramatic cursive *C* with an emerald at the top of it.

She held it up to examine it. It glinted in the light like a disco ball.

"Wow," Cassie said, almost breathless. Sheila

47

and Paul were great gift givers, but this was really special.

Sheila took it from Cassie and put it around her wrist, helping Cassie with the clasp.

"We thought this birthday was the beginning of so many new adventures in your life. And a charm bracelet is the perfect start to collecting memories."

"I love it," Cassie said, looking at it on her arm, and shaking her wrist a bit so the bracelet would move. The charm made a precious tinkling sound. Cassie jumped up and gave Sheila and Paul huge hugs.

As Sheila went to finish up breakfast, Paul slid a tiny box across the table.

"What's this?" Cassie asked, surprised that there was another gift. This box had Paul written all over, wrapped in silly Mickey Mouse paper, with a bright red, teeny-tiny bow on top. It wasn't nearly as nice a wrapping job as the other gift, but that made Cassie love it even more.

"Just a little something," he said.

Cassie smiled. She looked over at Sheila, who was beaming from next to the stove.

There was a little envelope on top. It was just a plain card with a note that read: *To my slugger. Love, Dad.* When Cassie was in third grade, she played Little League. She was one of the only girls in Houston to do it and it made Paul so proud. She was terrible but loved to play, and loved the time with Paul.

Cassie opened the box. She found a second charm inside. A tiny silver baseball bat. "This is so sweet!" she said, looking at the charm in the palm of her hand.

As Cassie attached it to her bracelet, Sheila came over with a huge pile of heart-shaped pancakes, covered in whipped cream and strawberries and blueberries. Heaven.

"I heart heart pancakes!" Cassie said.

Sheila sat down and they ate Thirteenth Birthday Breakfast together, to the sweet clinking sound of Cassie's charm bracelet.

CHAPTER 6

Well, This Is a Different Birthday

At Sam Houston, the girls would always decorate lockers for their birthdays. Last year, Cassie and Laura even found a way to put a little sound chip that played "Happy Birthday" in Erin's locker so when she opened it, music blared.

But this morning at Oak Grove was different. There were no balloons on Cassie's locker, no surprises inside. Cassie couldn't help feeling a little disappointed as she loaded in her books.

"Birthday girl!" Etoile called from down the hallway. She ran to Cassie and gave her a big hug. Etoile had already told Cassie that her extra-special BFF present would be coming later. "SO?"

Etoile asked, her eyes sparkling. "Are you having a good day so far?"

"Completely!" Cassie said, her spirits lifting immediately.

"You look amazing. That dress is perfect."

Cassie smiled. It was a new dress, bought especially for today. Green and high-waisted, with just a little ruffling at the neck and hem.

"How was dinner with the girls?" Etoile asked.

"Great. It was so nice to see Laura and Erin," Cassie said, deciding not to mention last night's initial weirdness to Etoile.

"I'm sure it was. I can't believe they're going to come to school this afternoon!" Etoile said, and Cassie was relieved to see that her friend seemed genuinely excited.

As Cassie stuffed a textbook in her bag, she heard the gentle tinkle of her charm bracelet.

"Oh!" she said. "How could I forget?" She held her wrist out to Etoile. "Look what Sheila and Paul got me!"

Etoile looked at the bracelet with big doe eyes. "Oh, it's so beautiful!"

Cassie pointed out the *C* and then the baseball bat.

"You played Little League?" Etoile asked, shocked.

"Yup. For two seasons. I kind of hated it but loved hanging out with Paul. And to freak all those little boys out."

"You were the only girl?"

"Totally!"

"Wow, there are so many things that I don't know about you," Etoile mused. "But this one is my new favorite!"

Cassie giggled. "Want to stop at the ladies' for a b-day touch-up before going to homeroom?"

"Totally," Etoile said.

Arm in arm, they walked to the ladies', Cassie ready to do her first gloss check as a thirteen-year-old.

When the lunch bell rang, Cassie met up with Etoile and walked to the cafeteria. The lunch table was always a great part of the day. And since the camping trip, Cassie and Etoile sat with Mary Ellen, Lynn, and Margery. Jonah and Seth often sat with them, too. As Cassie put her tray down on the table, Mary Ellen, Lynn, and Margery all wished her happy birthday.

"Wow, that bracelet is fantastic," Lynn said. She never missed a thing.

"I kind of love thinking about all the charms that will fill it up," Cassie said dreamily.

"But won't it get noisy then?" snipped Mary Ellen, always the downer.

Etoile gave Mary Ellen a nudge. "Sorry. I just mean . . ." Mary Ellen mumbled.

"I know what you mean, Mary Ellen," Cassie said, feathers unruffled. She and Mary Ellen understood each other these days.

Just then, Seth and Jonah approached.

"Yo!" Seth said, sitting next to Etoile, who turned her usual shade of pale. "Happy birthday, Cass!" He put his hand up for a high five.

"Thanks!" she said. Seth was teaching Cassie a special high-five routine and the two of them went through it slowly. Cassie always missed the third slap, which happened behind the back.

"You might need to practice a bit more," Seth pointed out.

"We're getting there!" Cassie laughed.

Jonah walked around the table and squeezed

himself in, right next to Cassie. He looked dashing in a black shirt and white tie and gray skinny jeans. With green Converses! Cassie wondered if he knew that green was her new color. She hoped so!

"Happy birthday," he said.

"Thanks!" Cassie said, trying not to glow too much in front of Etoile.

"How excited are you for tomorrow night?" Lynn asked Cassie as the group of friends began eating. Cassie was a little bit relieved *and* a little bit disappointed that she didn't have to talk to Jonah anymore.

"I can't wait!" Cassie answered truthfully. She hadn't been roller-skating since her days in Texas and she missed it so much. She'd invited the entire class, and now Erin and Laura would be special guest stars.

"And I can't wait to meet your friends from Texas!" Lynn said.

"They'll be here at four today if you're around to say hi," Cassie said, sipping her Vitaminwater.

Mary Ellen looked across the table at Cassie, concerned. "Do you think they're going to like Oak Grove?"

Cassie bit her lip. That hadn't occurred to her. "I think so! I mean, how could they not?"

"Well, you didn't like it when you first got here, so maybe you should be prepared."

Oh. Was Mary Ellen right? "I did like it!" Cassie protested. "It just took a little time to get used to."

Margery nudged Mary Ellen.

"Sorry," Mary Ellen said again.

"I know what you mean," Cassie said.

But by the time the warning bell rang, Cassie was officially nervous. Everyone gathered their gear and headed to afternoon classes.

Mary Ellen caught up with Cassie. "I'm sorry," she whispered. "I didn't mean to scare you or anything."

"No, I know," Cassie said. "But it's true that they might not like Oak Grove as much as we do. There's a lot that's different here."

"Yes. But *you* are here, too. That's a good thing." Mary Ellen smiled and Cassie did, too.

By the time Cassie headed to Yearbook at the end of the day, butterflies had officially set up camp in her stomach. Her two worlds were coming together and as excited as she was, she was also worried.

As Cassie walked down the hallway, her new green flats clicking against the shiny floor, she crashed into Mr. Blackwell, rushing out of the faculty lounge.

"Whoa!" he shouted, dropping his briefcase.

"Sorry!" Cassie cried, brought back to reality.

"Someone's in another galaxy, huh?" he asked.

Cassie laughed. "I guess I am."

"Everything okay?"

"Not sure yet," she said. Cassie knew she could tell Mr. B anything but she wasn't sure there was anything to tell yet.

"Well, if you figure it out, I'm around to talk." He smiled and Cassie felt relieved. She really liked the people at Oak Grove.

Cassie thanked Mr. B, and made sure he had all of his stuff back in his briefcase. Then he started down the hallway at a gallop. She wondered where he was rushing off to. Wouldn't they just head over to Yearbook together?

Cassie brushed away thoughts of Erin and Laura and focused on all she had to do in Yearbook that day. The committee had only two more sessions to get the final pages together so that it would print in time for the last school day. It had been a really busy few months, selecting just the right photos to represent all the big moments of the year.

Cassie and Etoile had thought the sports photos would prove to be the most difficult. But then, when they started on the club pages, they ran into an even bigger obstacle: Mary Ellen, the president of the American History Club. The original shot had been taken over a month ago. Mary Ellen looked pretty—it was hard for her not to, with her clear skin and sparkly eyes. But the girl never paid any attention to what she wore. Or to her hair. In the picture, it was in that dreadful ponytail! There was simply no way a friend of Cassie's could be seen in the yearbook with a scrunchie in her hair. So, after a month of lunchtime begging, Etoile and Cassie had been able to convince Mary Ellen to agree to a reshoot. They were going to see the new photo today and Cassie couldn't wait!

Cassie was just about to turn the knob when Etoile appeared out of nowhere.

"Hey! What are you doing?" she said.

"Etoile!" Cassie squealed. "You totally scared me! What are *you* doing?"

Etoile smoothed her hair. "Huh? Nothing? What?" She was standing in front of the Yearbook door, looking nutty.

"Well, then, let's go in. We have a ton of work to do before Erin and Laura get here." Cassie's stomach jumped when she said that.

"Okay," Etoile said loudly, "let's go in."

She stepped out of the way and allowed Cassie to walk in. The room was dark and empty.

Cassie looked around in confusion. "Etoile, what's . . ."

But before Cassie could finish, Etoile flipped the lights on and everyone on the Yearbook staff jumped out from behind the desks and roared, "Happy birthday!"

The surprise washed over her. Cassie looked at all of the smiling faces. Even Mr. B had made it, and he was holding a tray of mini cupcakes.

"How did you get here so fast?" Cassie asked her teacher, incredulous.

"I ran! I thought I'd ruined everything!" he laughed, shrugging.

"This is so nice of you guys," Cassie said, grinning from ear to ear. "Thank you so much, everyone!"

"Speech! Speech!" Jonah and Seth yelled from the back of the room.

Cassie blushed but regained her composure quickly. "This has been a crazy few months for me but now I really feel like I was meant to be here, in Maine, at Oak Grove, with y'all." She'd been able to catch a lot of her Texas talk in the past few months, especially since so many people made fun of it in her first days at the Grove. But Cassie knew when to use it for effect. This was SO one of those times. "And now," she concluded, "let's eat some cupcakes and get to work!"

Everyone laughed and dove for the cupcakes. As Cassie savored hers, Mr. B and Miss Hood walked around, doing final checks on the sections.

While Etoile headed to the storage room to pull some pages, Jonah walked over to Cassie. He held a small box wrapped in really loud pink paper.

"Um, hey, Cassie?" he said, and cleared his throat. "I just wanted to give you a little gift."

"Really?" she asked excitedly. She glanced around the room to make sure no one, especially Etoile, was watching.

Jonah handed her the gift and Cassie did her best not to tear it open. Remembering her Texas manners, she carefully tore the paper and opened the box. Inside, buried in red tissue paper, sat the ugliest headband Cassie had ever seen. Hot-pink and purple braided, with gold threading, and a checkered trim. It was awful!

Cassie took a deep breath. "This is the cutest headband ever!" she managed to say. She knew Jonah had meant well, and was touched by his thoughtfulness. She would have to figure out a way to wear the headband someday soon.

"I know you like stuff like that so I thought you might think this one was cool," Jonah mumbled, blushing from the neck up.

"I love it. Thank you!" Cassie said. She gave him a quick, awkward hug and then the two of them scurried off in opposite directions. Cassie stuffed the headband in her bag, then got to work.

Etoile walked over just as Cassie was bringing up the revised American History Club page on the computer.

"Okay, here's last pass," Etoile said, showing Cassie the old printout of Mary Ellen's picture.

60

The new page flashed up on the computer screen, and it was fantastic. Mary Ellen looked beautiful in her updated photo. Her hair—free from its scrunchie—glowed, her sweater flattered, and her smile sparkled.

"We *are* good!" Cassie said, high-fiving Etoile.

Cassie scanned the room for Mary Ellen and called her over.

"What's up?" Mary Ellen asked.

Etoile pointed to the screen. Mary Ellen's jaw dropped. "You guys are . . ." She stopped dramatically.

Cassie's heart sank. *What if she hates it?*

"THE BEST!" Mary Ellen exclaimed.

"You mean it?" Cassie asked, surprised.

She hesitated for a moment. "Yup," Mary Ellen said. "I owe you."

"I'm sure I'll take you up on that," Cassie laughed.

"I can't even imagine what that favor will be," Mary Ellen said, rolling her eyes and heading back to her workstation.

While she worked, Cassie kept her eye on the clock. As she and Etoile gave the pages last looks,

Cassie couldn't help but feel distracted by her Texas friends' impending arrival.

At 3:15, Cassie's phone buzzed with a text from Erin.

We're totally early. B there in a few! Sorrs!

"Oh no. They're going to be here any minute," Cassie said, concerned.

"Really?" Etoile asked. "We kind of have a lot more work to do."

"I know," Cassie sighed. "I should run down and meet them, though. Maybe they can hang out here while we finish up?"

"Sure," Etoile said. "Or you should just go and I'll finish up here."

Cassie considered this for a moment. "No," she decided. "They can hang out in here while we work. But come with me! They'll be disappointed if you're not there."

Etoile hesitated for a moment and then agreed. The girls explained to Mr. Blackwell that they would be back shortly. Then they headed to the ladies' for a quick hair check.

Bright sunlight slanted through the windows, as they examined themselves in the mirror. Cassie studied her still-straight red hair, the butterflies coming back.

"Are you sure I look okay, Cass?" Etoile asked. She was in one of her newest—and coolest—creations, a tartan-plaid jumper with a super-starched white shirt underneath.

"You look marvelous," Cassie said, fluffing one of the ruffles on her dress. "Okay, we should go," she added. The two girls gave each other big smiles and headed to the main entrance of the school.

CHAPTER 7
Hello, Texas!

As Cassie and Etoile walked outside, Cassie spotted Laura's dad's rental car in front of the school. Cassie waved at him, and he rolled down the window.

"Tell your folks I'll call them later for dinner," he called cheerily.

"I will!" Cassie said. "This is Etoile," she added.

"Howdy!" he called to Etoile, who waved awkwardly.

Then the car door opened and Erin and Laura tumbled out, their hair big and their outfits bright. They ran to Cassie, screaming "Happy birthday!" Etoile took a slight step back.

Laura reached into her purse and threw a handful of confetti at Cassie. The bright, sparkly flecks floated all around, landing on Cassie's hair and on the ground. Cassie immediately thought she should clean it up but didn't want to seem rude.

"Welcome to the Grove!" Cassie said, hugging her friends.

"Could it be any more gorgeous?" Laura asked, her eyes darting from side to side, taking it all in.

"And, guys," Cassie added dramatically, "this is Etoile!"

Both Erin and Laura squealed. "Well, it's about time we get to meet you in person!" Erin said.

Etoile stepped forward, a big smile plastered on her face. "You too!" She smoothed her hair quickly.

Laura leaned in and gave Etoile a huge hug. "I'm Laura!" she shouted in Etoile's ear.

"I know!" Etoile said, clearly trying to match Laura's enthusiasm.

"And I'm Erin." Cassie's Texas BFF extended her hand to Etoile in a slightly formal way. Etoile met her hand and they shook.

Cassie could see the three girls taking one another in and evaluating one another's outfits. They couldn't have been more different. If Etoile was all understated vintage chic, Erin and Laura were overstated and trendy. Cassie loved the Texas girls' looks, of course. But they did seem a little over the top compared to everyone—and everything—else at the Grove.

Erin spotted the charm bracelet and gasped. "Cass! Is that your gift from Sheila and Paul?"

Etoile cocked her head. "You call them Sheila and Paul, too?" She sounded annoyed, which Cassie didn't really understand.

"Totally!" Erin replied innocently. "Don't you?"

"No. I call them Mr. and Mrs. Knight. I thought only Cassie called them by their first names." Etoile looked disappointed.

"Oh, no, all the girls in Texas call them Sheila and Paul," Laura said dismissively. Then she looked back at the bracelet. "Isn't it precious?" she cooed.

"I love it. I knew you would, too!" Erin said to Cassie, beaming.

"Wait, how did you know about it?" Cassie asked.

"Oh, I have my ways," Erin grinned, satisfied.

"Did you know about *this*?" Cassie asked, showing the girls the baseball bat.

"Awwww!" Erin and Laura sighed in unison. "Cassie, the baseball star!"

"More like the baseball mess!" Cassie said.

"No! You were so awesome," Laura said. "We used to go to all the games and cheer her on," Laura explained to Etoile.

"That's cute," Etoile said, but she didn't smile.

"Cute nuthin'," Erin said. "We had to support our girl!"

"So, would you guys mind coming to Yearbook for a while?" Cassie asked the new arrivals. "We have some more work to do."

"Not at all! It'll be like being back in Houston," Laura said. "Sorry we're so early. My dad thought it would take a lot longer to get here."

"Don't worry about it," Cassie said, leading the way into the main building.

As they walked back to Yearbook, Cassie and Etoile showed Erin and Laura some Oak Grove highlights. First their wooden lockers, which was where Etoile and Cassie had first met. Next stop was the caf, which made Erin and Laura very jealous because the food sounded better than what they got in Houston; and then the theater, where the details of the Fash Bash were discussed in great detail.

"I can't wait to meet Mary Ellen!" Laura said. "She might need a little Texas Tude from me!"

"No, no—she doesn't," Cassie said. "We're good now. We're friends."

"Friends? Or frenemies?" Erin asked.

Cassie looked at Etoile. "Well?"

"To be determined," Etoile said with a raised eyebrow.

"Well, *we* don't like her—" Laura said.

Etoile cut her off. "No, you should really give her a chance; she's a nice person."

Laura rolled her eyes.

When they got to the Yearbook room, the rest of the staff looked up curiously.

"Everyone, these are my closest friends from Texas, Erin and Laura," Cassie announced.

"Hey, y'all," Erin said.

Everyone muttered hellos and went back to work. Someone at the back of the room mockingly said, "Hey, y'all," and the room erupted into laughter. Erin and Laura blushed, but kept smiles on their faces.

Cassie had flashbacks to her first uncomfortable days at Oak Grove.

"Guys," Mr. Blackwell said forcefully. He looked at Cassie and the girls. "Welcome, Erin and Laura," he said warmly. "Today is actually a major deadline for us, so if you don't mind rolling up your sleeves a little, we can use all the help we can get."

Erin and Laura wanted to help out, so Cassie and Etoile led them to their workstation. They spent the next half hour looking through photos and even though Etoile seemed a bit territorial, she listened to Erin's and Laura's suggestions, nodding and smiling. Cassie could see that it wasn't Etoile's genuine smile, but the Texas girls didn't know that, she hoped. With Erin's and Laura's help, they got through the work quickly, and soon were ready to leave.

Mary Ellen had her nose buried in her work the whole time, and Cassie didn't want to disturb her. But she did want her to meet the Texas girls. So as she and Etoile packed up their things, Cassie called Mary Ellen over.

"Erin and Laura, this is Mary Ellen!" Cassie smiled as the girls shook hands.

"Nice to meet you," Mary Ellen said warmly. "I've heard a lot about you."

"Oh, not as much as we've heard about you, I'm sure," Laura said sarcastically.

Cassie's eyes bugged out of her head in annoyance. *Did she really just say that?* Cassie wondered.

"Well," Mary Ellen said uncomfortably, "I'll see you around." She bit her lip, and said good-bye to Cassie and Etoile.

"That was rude," Etoile said to Laura, her voice tight, as soon as Mary Ellen was out of earshot.

"Not as rude as she was to Cassie!" Erin said.

"It's ancient history now, I've told you that," Cassie said, rushing them out of Yearbook. She needed a change of scenery.

Cassie continued the tour through the hall-ways, into the language lab, the gym, and of course, a special trip to Principal Veronica's office. (Earlier in the day, Cassie had asked if it would be okay for them to stop by and say hello.) Both Erin and Laura were chewing gum and Cassie asked them to get rid of it before meeting PV. She was a stickler for manners.

"Really?" Erin asked, snapping her gum.

"I know, I'm sorry. It's just that PV hates gum chewing," Cassie said.

"Whatever," Erin said, putting her gum in a tissue.

"But this is a new piece," Laura said.

"You should just get rid of it," Etoile insisted.

Laura rolled her eyes but took out her piece of gum as well.

Cassie knocked on the door and PV came out to greet them. She was in her uniform. That's what Cassie and Etoile called it: a gray suit with a white blouse underneath, an Oak Grove pin on her lapel, and her gray hair in a bun.

"Girls, come in, please!" she said gracefully.

"Principal Veronica, these are my friends from Texas who I was telling you about. Erin and Laura, this is Principal Veronica." Both girls extended their hands to say hello.

"How wonderful that you've come to visit the campus. Are Cassie and Etoile giving you a good tour?"

"Oh yes," Erin said, sounding slightly nervous and formal. "It's just . . . precious here."

"Thank you. Your state is a lovely one, as well."

"It's pretty cute," Laura said with a giggle.

Cassie leaned forward slightly. "We were just wrapping up, and I wanted to make sure you all had a chance to meet." She felt warm now with nervousness.

"I'm very glad we did," PV said.

"Well, we'll leave you to your work," Cassie said, slowly backing up. Erin and Laura shook PV's hand again and as they turned to leave, PV said, "Happy birthday, Cassie. I hear you're having a roller-skating party this weekend?"

"Yes, I am! Would you like to come?" Cassie asked sincerely. Principal Veronica was one cool lady and Cassie would have adored skating with her.

Erin and Laura laughed, which made Cassie tense up even more. She hoped PV wouldn't think the girls were laughing at *her*.

Without hesitation, PV laughed, too. "That's very kind of you, but I haven't roller-skated since I was your age. I don't think I'd be very good. Thank you for the invitation, though!"

"You're welcome. Have a good weekend!" Cassie said.

"It was nice to meet you," Erin said, the word "you" coming out as "yeeew."

Laura said the same and even did a strange little curtsy as they walked out of the office. Cassie wasn't positive but she thought she saw Etoile rolling her eyes.

They walked out of the office, Cassie's heart beating fast.

When they were down the hallway, Etoile turned to Cassie. "How awesome is she? Imagine if she'd really come to your party!"

Before Cassie could answer, Laura jumped in. "She seems okay. But that office? Could it be more drab?"

Erin was right behind her. "And her hair? Not to mention that suit. BORING!"

Cassie didn't know what to say. She'd thought the exact same things when she first met PV, but she certainly didn't feel that way now. She looked at Etoile. It seemed like she wanted to say something but when she caught Cassie's eye, she stopped herself.

"And I can't believe you invited her skating. Are you becoming a nerd or what?" Laura asked.

Etoile hated the nerd word. "What's nerdy about being gracious?" she asked.

They walked down the hall quietly for a while then.

"Sheila is going to be here any minute," Cassie said. "We should grab our stuff and get to the driveway."

As they stood waiting for Sheila to arrive, they were silent. Cassie searched for something to say that wouldn't exclude Etoile. Or something to say that wouldn't alienate Erin and Laura. Nothing came. She forced herself to be okay with the lapse in conversation. And just as she found that place, the unthinkable happened: The lacrosse team came walking over the lawn from practice. They didn't have lacrosse at Sam Houston, and Cassie remembered thinking it seemed like such an odd sport when she first learned about it.

"Ooh, boy alert!" Laura said.

Cassie turned. She'd never heard Laura say something quite so silly. "Boy alert?"

Erin wrinkled her nose. "What kind of weird sport is that?"

"It's lacrosse," Etoile said. She'd had the same conversation with Cassie just a handful of months ago.

"La-who?" Laura asked, a slight edge to her voice.

"Lacrosse. It's like playing catch with little nets on sticks," Cassie said, hoping she was at least a little bit right.

"That sounds dumb," Erin said, staring at the approaching boys.

Just then, Brian Clark, the captain of the team, walked over to say hi to Etoile and Cassie.

"Brian, these are Cassie's friends from Texas, Erin and Laura," Etoile said.

"Nice to meet *yeeew*," they both crooned. Even Cassie rolled her eyes with that one.

"Whoa," he said. "You really *are* from Texas, huh?" He laughed at his own silly joke.

"Well, what does that mean?" Erin asked.

"Nothing, I was . . ." Brian froze then. "I was just . . ."

Cassie knew Brian was just being silly. "He was kidding," she said firmly. She'd been through enough of this type of teasing when she first arrived to know the difference between good fun and mockery.

"Because Cassie is from Texas, too. Unless she's forgotten that?" Laura asked.

"How could I forget that?" Cassie asked. "Brian, you're coming to the skating party on Saturday, right?"

"Of course," he said happily.

Silence. Again.

"Well, I'll see you then. Nice to meet you guys," he said. He ran to join his teammates.

"Is everyone snobby like that here?" Erin asked flatly.

"He's not a snob at all. He was just giving you a hard time. Seriously," Cassie said.

As if sent by an angel, Sheila's car pulled into the wide main driveway of the school. Cassie felt relieved to be leaving the campus and to have her mother in the mix. She hoped it would help.

CHAPTER 8

Color War

"Sheila!" Erin shouted.

Cassie's mom jumped out of the car and excitedly hugged Erin and Laura.

"I love your hair!" Laura said. Since they'd been in Maine, Sheila had gone from long, caramel highlights to a blunt, chic, brown bob. It had been a big step, but with Cassie by her side, she'd done it. Both of them agreed that change was a good thing. So while Cassie adjusted to Oak Grove, Sheila cut a bob. And what a wise choice it was.

They piled into the car, Etoile offering to sit in the front so Cassie could be in back with the Texas girls. Cassie resisted at first but then sat in the back. She knew Etoile was trying hard to make the afternoon as easy as possible but she was already feeling bad about things.

As they drove, Sheila asked the girls a bunch of questions about Houston. Cassie couldn't believe how familiar it felt to be driving home from school with Erin and Laura. Like no time had passed at all.

"How's Ritchie's? You guys still go all the time with your folks?" Sheila asked, looking at Erin and Laura in the rearview.

"NO!" Erin said passionately. "My mom didn't tell you?"

Together, Sheila and Cassie gasped. "Tell us what?"

Erin and Laura looked at one another. "I can't even say it," Erin said. "You tell."

"Okay, well," Laura said, "one night when we were there, the guy sitting at the table next to ours found a huge palmetto bug in his salad."

Sheila gasped from the front seat.

"No way!" Cassie yelled, half grossed out and half fascinated. "What did he do?"

Erin picked up the story. "He actually jumped up and knocked his chair over and screamed."

"No!" Cassie yelled.

"Oh, wait! Duh! Do you know who the guy was?" Erin asked.

"Who?" Sheila squealed.

"Donny McMahill's dad!" Erin said.

"James McMahill jumped and screamed over a palmetto bug?" Sheila said, laughing hysterically now. "I can't wait to tell Paul this."

Everyone in the car laughed and laughed. Except for Etoile. When Cassie realized this, she tried her best to explain. "Etoile, Ritchie's is this awesome restaurant near home—in Houston—and James McMahill is Donny's dad. Donny's in our class—their class—and he's like a big jock guy—"

"And has taken over as class prez since you left us," Laura said.

Sheila picked up, "Mr. McMahill is always in a tracksuit, always looks like he just lifted weights. A real macho guy. I wish I could have seen that! What did your parents do?"

"My mom totally jumped up and asked him if he was okay and offered him ice water," Laura said. "I can't believe she didn't tell you this!"

"I know!" Sheila said.

"What's a palmetto bug?" Etoile asked softly.

"You guys don't have them here?" Erin asked incredulously.

"Um, no," Etoile said.

"They're big, gross, flying cockroaches," Sheila said, her face twisted in disgust.

"I can't believe you don't have them here!" Erin said. "You guys have it easy!"

They turned onto Deer Run Drive. "Okay, guys, this is our street," Cassie said.

Erin and Laura turned to the window quickly to see.

"Wow, so many trees. It's crazy!" Laura said.

"What are those bushes?" Erin asked.

"Blueberries," Etoile said from the front seat.

"Really? Like, real blueberry bushes?" Erin asked, surprised.

"Yup," Etoile said sharply. *"Like, real blueberry bushes."*

Cassie shot Etoile an annoyed look, and wondered if she had said it that way on purpose.

They turned into Cassie's driveway then and got out of the car. Erin and Laura grabbed their bags from the trunk and followed Cassie and Etoile to the house.

"Wow, so when you say you're on the lawn, you really mean the lawn!" Erin said, taking in the sizable front yard.

"Don't you guys have lawns?" Etoile asked.

"Of course we do. Just not this big is all," Laura said with the slightest bit of extra Texas twang.

Sheila had a little snack waiting for them inside, so the girls stood in the kitchen, munching on cheese and crackers and chatting. Things were feeling smoother now that they were on Cassie's turf. She knew everyone was nervous. She let that all wash away now. There were a lot of exciting things for them to do together.

"Okay, time for another tour!" Cassie said.

As they walked through the house, Cassie pointed out her favorite things. The way the third stair on the staircase squeaked, the wood paneling on the den wall, the pine tree outside the living room window that was almost growing through the window. All of these things were so Maine, and so cool to Cassie. But Erin and Laura didn't seem too interested in seeing anything but Cassie's room.

As they approached her bedroom, Cassie

warned Erin and Laura. "Get ready. This is a big change from my last room, so be prepared."

"Okay," the girls said, their tones overly dramatic.

Cassie opened the door to her chocolate and white room and let them walk in first. They were quiet, taking it all in. Laura saw a picture of the trio in Texas and walked over to it. She plucked it off the wall and handed it to Erin, smiling.

"SO?" Cassie asked.

"It's so different," Erin said.

"I know. It's like the color police came and arrested all the colors," Laura said.

"What? Really? There's color," Cassie said, pointing to the red leather journal on her desk. "And there," pointing to the leopard picture frame. "Pops of color everywhere!" Cassie said nervously.

"It's adorable, really," Erin said. "It's just different from before. I hadn't been able to see the whole room from our chats."

"Yeah, I guess it is pretty different," Cassie said, slightly melancholy.

"Well, I love it," Etoile spoke up, smoothing her brown hair. "It's simple and understated. Elegant. That's a really good thing."

"I know," said Erin. "I just said it was different."

There was a chilly moment among the four girls until Cassie turned on her iTunes. One of her favorite Beyoncé songs came on.

"Okay," she said, knowing what would bond the girls for sure. "I have some outfit questions for tomorrow."

"Fashion show!" Erin sang, clapping.

"I wish you guys could have been at the Fash Bash," Cassie said, pulling things out of the closet. "We had so much fun."

"It was awesome," Etoile nodded, but Laura and Erin didn't seem interested in hearing about the Fash Bash again.

Cassie hung three outfits on the closet door and held them up, one at a time. They were all new purchases since she'd been in Maine. One was a dress with green polka dots against navy blue, another a black tank dress with a camel-colored trim, and the third, an adorable Harajuku Lovers printed shirt and matching shorts.

"These are the options for your big skating party?" Erin asked, disappointed.

"Yeah. I think so. Why?" Cassie asked, looking at the clothes.

"They're cute and all," Laura said, "but they're just kind of boring."

"Cassie Cyan Knight would never have been caught dead in those things at her roller-skating party in Texas!" Erin said.

"What do you mean?" Etoile asked.

"I just mean, the Cassie that we know would have had leg warmers on and a frilly skirt and some real color! She would have worn a vintage Swatch in her hair! Not dressed like she was going to a school concert or something."

Cassie began to second-guess her outfits.

"Well, the Cassie I know would definitely wear any of these outfits with style and grace!" Etoile said emphatically.

Cassie stood, looking from Etoile to Erin, confused and upset.

"Well, I can keep looking at the mall today, maybe?" Cassie said, trying to maintain the peace.

"For what? More boring clothes? It seems like you have plenty of those already," Laura said, trying to make a joke. But it landed painfully. Cassie stood, staring at the girls. Another silence fell over them.

Just then, Sheila called from downstairs.

"It's time to get ready to go to the mall!" she said. "You guys doing okay?"

"Yes, we're good," Cassie yelled from her room. But looking at Erin's, Laura's, and Etoile's sour pusses, Cassie wasn't so sure.

CHAPTER 9

Mall Meltdown

"So, should we start with manis and pedis?" Cassie asked as they walked into the bustling mall. "Or maybe an Auntie Anne's pretzel?"

"Pah-retzel! Totally!" Laura said. Erin and Etoile were silent.

Cassie led them to the pretzel stand and they got two different pretzels to split. As the buttery twists passed back and forth between the girls, Cassie noticed that Etoile and Erin weren't sharing with each other. They weren't even looking at each other!

A woman with a tiny dog in her arms walked by. "Look at that puppy!" Cassie said, hoping to lighten the mood. "It's so adorable."

"Like Snoodle!" Laura said.

"Etoile, Erin has the cutest little dog," Cassie said, hoping for a connection.

"I know," Etoile said calmly. "I've seen it in pictures."

"He," Erin said. "Snoodle is a *he*, not an it."

"Sorry. I've seen *him* in pictures," Etoile said. She got up from the bench then. "Okay, let's go get our nails done, y'all."

Cassie was used to hearing Etoile say "y'all." She'd picked it up from Sheila, and Cassie thought it was the sweetest thing ever.

But Erin didn't seem to think so. "Are you making fun of us?" Erin asked, her face angry and her eyebrows pointed skyward.

"What?" Etoile asked, surprised. "How?"

"Erin, Etoile says that all the time," Cassie interrupted.

"Oh," Erin said, but she didn't look convinced. She walked away then.

A few minutes later, the four girls sat in a lineup at the nail salon, reading magazines, while their feet were scrubbed, buffed, and soaked. To an outsider, Cassie imagined, everything looked fine. But she knew the story was very different.

Erin's phone beeped and she pulled it out of her purse to take a look.

"No way!" she said when she read the text.

"What?" Laura asked excitedly.

Erin flushed. "Oh, it's nothing. It's just . . ."

Cassie leaned forward, throwing her magazine on her lap. "Spill."

"I know what it is," Laura said.

"Then tell us!" Cassie said, laughing.

"It's a text from Donny."

"MCMAHILL!?" Cassie asked.

Erin flushed.

"Wait, the class president whose dad screamed at the *palomino* bug?" Etoile asked.

"*Palmetto* bug," Cassie corrected her friend, distracted. Then she turned back to Erin.

"Excuse me, lady, what's up with Donny texting you?"

Erin's eyes were sparkling. "Nothing. At all. Really. We worked on a class project together and became sort of friends."

"No. WAY!!" Cassie shrieked. "Etoile, he is supercute and really popular."

"He's not *that* cute," Erin said, still blushing.

"Yes, he is!" Laura said.

"Well, what about you, Cassie?" Laura asked. "Any birthday texts from *your* guy?"

Cassie froze. *Jonah.* She didn't think he'd come up in conversation, especially since he hadn't been at Yearbook when the girls came.

"What guy?" Etoile asked, her face somewhere between confused and upset.

"No one. They're just being silly," Cassie said, feeling nervous.

"Silly?" Laura asked. "Every time you get an IM from him while you're talking to us you turn bright red!"

"He even has a cute name," Erin said. "What is it? Justin?"

Etoile turned to Cassie. "JONAH?"

"That's it!" Erin said.

"It's nothing," Cassie protested, squirming in her chair and almost messing up the polish on her toes. "Sometimes I think he's cute. That's all."

"How come I don't know this?" Etoile asked quietly. It was clear she was hurt, and Cassie felt awful.

"It's nothing. I swear. I didn't want to say anything because he's practically your brother," Cassie said pleadingly.

"But you told *them*," Etoile said, disappointed.

Just then the four women that were polishing the girls' toenails told them it was time to sit down at the manicure stations. They slid their paper slippers on and headed to the front of the salon. Cassie's feet were feeling good. But nothing else was. She should never have kept her crush on Jonah from Etoile for so long. And why had Laura and Erin blabbed, after Cassie swore them to secrecy?

Life Rule #71: Sooner or later, the lie is harder than the truth.

As the girls walked over, they all stopped at the polish bar to choose a color.

"I'm sorry I didn't tell you about Jonah," Cassie said quietly to Etoile.

"It's fine," Etoile said dismissively, looking intently at the shiny bottles.

"Etoile, it's not. I royally messed up," she said, her heart squeezing. She wished her friend would at least look at her.

"I don't want to talk about this right now,"

Etoile said, walking to the other side of the counter and picking up a bottle of Ballet Slippers.

Erin walked over, unknowingly interrupting them. "Okay, this one is it!" She held up a blue bottle: Tubular Teal.

"Not for me!" Cassie said. "I'm going green." She picked up a bottle of Green with Envy.

"Cass! Are you sure you're really giving up on teal? Just a few months ago, you wouldn't have been able to resist this color!" Laura said.

Cassie smiled. "Green feels more me lately."

"Well, we're still getting teal. In honor of the Cassie we know and love," Erin said firmly, with a flip of her blond hair.

"You should get teal," Etoile spoke up, but her tone was cold and distant. "They're getting it."

"No, this is good, thanks." It made Cassie happy that Etoile at least spoke to her, but she still felt terrible about the Jonah thing. She couldn't care less about nail polish now. Her thoughts spinning, she walked to the manicure station, leaving the three girls behind.

The manicures were mostly silent. Every now and then, one of the girls would ask a question or comment on a song on the radio. And when Cassie realized that Laura was having glitter butterflies painted on each of her nails, she began to worry that they would take too long and not have any time to eat dinner before Sheila picked them up. No matter what she did, Cassie couldn't find a happy medium. All day she'd hoped to find one but as the hours ticked by, it became evident: There remained a great divide between Texas and Maine.

When they were finally seated at Friendly's, Cassie's absolute favorite restaurant at the mall, she hoped they'd be able to relax. But the tension kept creeping up higher and higher.

Right after the waitress took their orders, Erin reached into her enormous zebra-striped bag and plunked the Sam Houston yearbook down on the table.

"Oh," Cassie said nervously, "you brought the yearbook?" This was going to be the end of Etoile, Cassie was certain.

"Um, yeah!" Erin squealed. "We just got them." She opened the book and flipped pages, landing on the Drama Club page. Smack dab in the center of the spread was a picture of the fall production of *Annie*.

"Look!" Erin exclaimed, pointing.

Cassie couldn't help her excitement. She jumped out of her seat to huddle around the yearbook with Erin and Laura. There they were, all of her favorite Texas girls, on stage, smiling. Cassie played Annie. Erin was a brilliant Miss Hannigan. And Laura was an adorable Pepper.

"They put it in!" Cassie said, her eyes filling with a few nostalgic tears. Paul had built the sets and Sheila was on the costume team. It was one of the best memories Cassie had of Houston.

Etoile stood up and leaned over the table, smiling tightly.

"Etoile! These are pictures from the show that I was telling you about!" Cassie said, turning the yearbook around so her friend could see.

"Cute," Etoile said, but before she could get a closer look, Erin flipped the page again. She turned to the masthead, and pointed to where Cassie was listed as photo editor.

"I didn't know you did Yearbook in Houston, too," Etoile said.

"Really? I thought you did. That's why I do it

here," Cassie said. She was sure she'd told Etoile that! Or maybe it had slipped her mind?

"Oh." Etoile sat down, looking defeated.

Cassie cleared her throat, feeling stupid once again. She'd imagined this evening as a blast — girl talk and laughter and fun moments. Instead, it felt more like a nightmare.

The food came then, but Cassie couldn't even enjoy her burger and extra-crispy fries. The girls ate quietly, the clanks of their forks and knives the only thing Cassie heard. When the waitress came back to clear their plates, Cassie was almost relieved.

Erin quickly excused herself to go to the ladies', bringing her enormous makeup bag with her. Laura, Cassie, and Etoile sat there for a moment, and then Etoile glanced at the yearbook again.

Laura took a sip of iced tea, and finally spoke. "Yeah, Erin and I used to do photos with Cassie. Now we do ads," she said.

Etoile sat up straighter, interested. "Really? I was wondering about ads. I kind of want to try that section, maybe next year."

Laura spoke a bit about the ads in the back and how she and Erin went to local restaurants and businesses to get them. When Erin returned from the ladies', she chimed in with stories of the best ads they had secured from the shops at the Houston Galleria mall.

"I think maybe I'm too shy for that part," Etoile said. "When we did the Fash Bash, Cassie did most of the talking to the stores about clothing donations."

Erin and Laura stared at Etoile for a moment. "Yeah, I was thinking it might not be the best job for you," Laura said coolly. She picked up the menu then. "Are we getting dessert?" she asked.

Etoile's face dropped. She looked hurt and angry. She picked up her menu and looked down at it for a moment. And then, in a voice that Cassie had never quite heard before, she asked, "What is your problem?"

Cassie's stomach fell. *Oh no*, she thought. This couldn't be happening!

Erin and Laura looked up from their menus, shocked. "Excuse me?" Erin asked.

Etoile's face was red now and her eyes were wide. "Ever since I've said hello to you two, all you've done is make me feel like an outsider."

Cassie gasped, and glanced at Erin and Laura to see if they would apologize.

No such luck.

"Because you are," Erin said, with a self-satisfied tone. "I'm sorry, Etoile, but you're *not* one of us."

Cassie felt like she was sinking in quicksand. She couldn't figure out how to get them out of this. "Guys, come on," she said gently. "We're in Friendly's! Get it? *Friendly's*?"

But her friends ignored her.

"I am not an outsider!" Etoile snapped back, her face growing redder by the second. "You are in our state now. You are visiting *us*!" Her voice cracked on the last word, and her eyes filled with tears. Cassie felt a pang at the sight.

"We aren't visiting you, we're visiting Cassie. You're just along for the ride," Laura retorted, glaring at Etoile.

"Erin! Laura! Stop!" Cassie said, so upset she thought *she* might cry.

Big tears fell from Etoile's eyes, and she didn't

bother to wipe them away. "Oh, please, Cassie," she managed to say through her tears. "Don't bother defending me. It's true. I thought we knew so much about each other but it's clear that we don't."

"We do. And the stuff we don't know, we're learning. That's what friends do!" Cassie said pleadingly, hoping this would all just go away.

"But what about Jonah?" Etoile demanded. "That's a big deal! When were you going to tell me?" she asked, holding back a sob. She put her hand over her mouth.

Cassie sat quietly. She didn't know how to answer.

"*We've* known for a long time," Laura said. She and Erin didn't even look sorry that Etoile was crying.

Cassie put her head in her hands in frustration. "Enough!" she cried.

"You know, I just don't understand," Erin said, her face twisted in annoyance. "We've been in Cassie's life a lot longer than you and for some reason, you just don't get that or something?" Her words were sharp.

Just then, the waitress came over with a big ice-cream sundae, topped with whipped cream and a candle. Erin must have told her to bring it over when she went to the ladies'. Normally, Cassie would have been delighted by her friends being so thoughtful, but instead she just wanted to burst into tears.

The waitress began singing "Happy Birthday" but when no one joined her, she stopped, looked around uncomfortably at the girls, and put the sundae on the table. "Happy birthday, dear," she said and walked away.

Cassie sat there, the candle burning lower and lower. She looked at her unhappy friends. Etoile was wiping her eyes with a napkin, attempting to pull herself together. Erin and Laura were sitting with their arms crossed over their chests, their jaws set. Cassie sighed and made the only wish she could.

I wish they would stop fighting. I wish Maine and Texas would be friends.

She smiled at the girls. "Thanks for the sundae, guys," she said quietly, trying her hardest to be sincere.

She closed her eyes.

She chanted in her head: *Just get along. Get along. Understand that each one of you is the best person on the planet.*

She blew the candle out and the girls clapped weakly.

Would her wish come true?

CHAPTER 10

Something's Gotta Give

"Cass," Sheila said, the car quiet, "why don't you put the radio on?"

Cassie, barely paying attention, flicked on the knob. She didn't fuss with the tuner, like she normally did, to find one of her favorite songs. A baseball game buzzed over the speakers.

"You guys like to listen to the baseball game now?" Sheila asked.

Silence from the girls in the backseat.

"No," Cassie said, quickly trying to cover. She didn't want anyone to know that they were all arguing. She flipped to a new station.

Sheila was driving the Texas girls back to their hotel, and then dropping Etoile off at home. Cassie was relieved—and not surprised—that no one had asked if they could sleep over at Cassie's house. She couldn't believe she was thinking this, but she just couldn't imagine spending any more time with the girls. Not after what had happened at Friendly's.

It was official: Cassie's thirteenth birthday felt more and more like a disaster.

They pulled up to the hotel. Laura's dad had eaten dinner with Sheila and Paul earlier, and now the dads waited for the girls at the front door.

Cassie stepped out of the car to say good-bye to Erin and Laura, although she could barely look at them.

"I don't think we should come to the party tomorrow," Erin said coldly.

"What? Why not?" Cassie asked, shocked and sad.

"Etoile doesn't want us there. And we definitely don't want to be around her," Erin said.

Laura shook her head.

"You feel this way, too?" Cassie asked Laura.

"Yes. She's totally rude. And jealous." Laura crossed her arms.

"Good night," Erin said. She didn't even hug

Cassie good-bye. She just walked into the hotel. Laura followed.

Stunned, Cassie got into the backseat with Etoile so Paul could sit up front.

More silence.

"How was your night?" Paul asked unknowingly.

"Great," Cassie said.

"Perfect," Etoile replied sarcastically, her arms crossed. She stared out the window at the road. Cassie wondered if she'd heard what Erin and Laura had said outside the hotel.

The drive was only fifteen minutes but it felt like hours. When they finally pulled into Etoile's driveway, Cassie tried to think of something to say but nothing came. "Have a good night," was all she could muster. She wanted to add that she was sorry about the Jonah thing but didn't want to say that in front of her parents.

"You too. Happy birthday," Etoile said curtly, opening the door. "I think I should skip the party tomorrow," she added quietly.

Not Etoile, too! Cassie thought.

"No, that's crazy. It's all going to be fine," Cassie said.

"I'm not sure about that," Etoile answered gravely. She cleared her throat, thanked Sheila and Paul, and walked to her front door.

Cassie plunked back into her seat, defeated.

"Are you going to tell us what happened?" Paul asked as they drove to their house.

"Nothing happened," Cassie lied.

"Cassie, please," Sheila said, looking at her through the rearview mirror.

"Okay, fine. This might have been the worst birthday ever." Cassie tried her best not to cry.

Sheila's face twisted up in that "let me fix the world for you" way that Cassie loved. "I was wondering why no one was sleeping over."

"No one asked to. They hate each other. And they hate me, I think." Tears dropped heavily down Cassie's cheeks. She held her phone in her hands, hoping someone would text.

"I'm sure they don't hate each other. And they certainly don't hate you," Paul said. "Cass, you're unhatable. And I don't just have to say that because you're my kid."

"They do. I should cancel the party, maybe," Cassie said, wiping the tears from her face. "They all said they don't even want to come!"

"Well, that seems a bit extreme," Paul said calmly.

Cassie shook her head. "I just don't think things can work out at this point," she admitted.

As they pulled the car into the garage, Sheila asked, "Want to eat some ice cream and watch TV?" This was Cassie's favorite Sheila prescription.

"That would be great," Cassie said gratefully. She'd barely touched her sundae, so ice cream sounded perfect.

Paul said good night then and went upstairs.

And so they sat, mother and daughter, side by side, flipping channels and giggling every now and then, the pint of Rocky Road passing back and forth between them.

When it was late, and the ice cream was long gone, they both decided to turn in.

"Before you put your head on the pillow, I want to say one thing," Sheila said.

Cassie looked at her mother, excited and nervous.

"Turning thirteen is a big step in a girl's life. And I know these past couple of days haven't been easy. But you're well on your way to becoming an adult — and all of your friends are, too."

Cassie nodded her head.

"Tomorrow is your big day. And I know those girls want nothing more than to see you happy," Sheila said.

"So what should I do?" Cassie asked, her eyes big.

"I wish I could tell you. But *I* don't even know." Sheila smiled. "Sleep on it. Tomorrow, you'll know."

She kissed Cassie on the head and gave her a big hug. "Happy birthday, Cass. Tomorrow is going to be a great day."

And even though Cassie wasn't sure what she would do to make it great, she knew her mother was right.

Cassie woke up too early for a Saturday morning. She'd slept surprisingly well, but when her eyes opened at nine, her next move wasn't clear. She got out of bed and opened her curtains. The sun was strong through the trees.

She paced around her room, something she did very well when she had to think things through.

She wondered what all the fighting was about, and how to best fix it. If a friend had come to her with this exact same problem, Cassie was certain she'd be able to help. But sitting in the middle of it all, nothing was clear. She wished she could talk to someone like Mr. Blackwell or Principal Veronica, but they wouldn't really get it.

Cassie plopped onto her bed and grabbed Bob the Bear.

"What do I do?" she asked him, realizing how silly she must have looked. She sat up then. Music might help. She walked to her laptop. As she did so, she stopped and looked at all her pics on the mirror. Her eye landed on the one of herself with Etoile and Mary Ellen at the camping trip.

Mary Ellen: the perfect choice for help?

Although they'd had their ups and downs, and arguments and attitudes, Mary Ellen was a good person. Logical and smart. It was Mary Ellen, after all, who got Cassie to take that bungee jump on the camping trip. And Mary Ellen who turned to Cassie when she needed help with the final night camping party.

Cassie grabbed her phone and sat down on the

bed. She texted Mary Ellen quickly, not allowing herself to think too much about it.

Hi. It's Cass. U up?

She threw the phone on to the bed and walked back to her laptop but before she could even turn it on, her phone was jingling. It was Mary Ellen, sure enough. Cassie cleared her throat and answered.

"I didn't think people besides me got up this early on the weekend," Mary Ellen said.

Of course Mary Ellen would be an early riser! *She probably sets her alarm on Saturdays so she can finish her homework,* Cassie thought.

"It just depends." Cassie had a little quiver in her voice.

"So, what's up?" Mary Ellen asked.

They rarely spoke on the phone, so this felt odd for both of them, Cassie was certain. "I don't know where to start," she said, her nerves riding high.

"Just start from the beginning," Mary Ellen said, her voice kind and steady.

"Nothing is working with Etoile and my friends from Texas," Cassie blurted.

Mary Ellen sighed. "Wow. I wondered how it was all going."

"Terribly." Cassie told Mary Ellen all about the previous night's drama, from all the little snipes to the full-blown fight at Friendly's.

"What should I do?" Cassie finished, flabbergasted.

Mary Ellen was quiet for a second, clearly thinking. "You don't have to do much. I guess, first of all, you need to get over the fact that the whole world is supposed to be . . ." She hesitated then and continued awkwardly. ". . . BFFs. Not everyone has to hold hands and love one another, you know. That's just not how life goes."

Cassie didn't know what to say. Was it wrong that she just wanted people to come together and be friends? "Oh," she muttered.

"I'm sorry," Mary Ellen said, "it's sort of true. But that's another conversation for another day."

Cassie closed her eyes. Her weekend of fun was crumbling around her. "Do you think I should cancel the party?" she asked.

"I'd love it if you did," Mary Ellen said teasingly. "I hate skating."

Cassie laughed a little. "I'm serious," she said.

"No, you should absolutely not cancel this party. There are a lot of people who want to celebrate with you," Mary Ellen said.

"I don't know. This could be so bad, though. What if they all fight again? Or don't show up?"

Mary Ellen sighed loudly. "Stop. Here's the thing: These girls need to get it together. This is your birthday. They adore you. And that's that."

"So what do I do?" Cassie asked.

"Nothing. You let me handle it."

"What? How?" Cassie asked, surprised.

"Don't worry about it," Mary Ellen said confidently.

"Well, they're all supposed to come over here later today to get ready for skating," Cassie said. "But at this point, I don't even know if they will."

"Great. I'm inviting myself over, if that's okay. And Lynn and Margery. Is that all right with you?"

For a moment, Cassie felt badly that she hadn't thought to invite Mary Ellen and her friends to join in the pre-party activities.

"And don't start feeling bad that you didn't invite us," Mary Ellen said, as if she were psychic.

"How did you know?" Cassie asked, slightly embarrassed.

"Cassie, please. You are such an easy read!" Mary Ellen said.

Cassie laughed. "Okay, so of course you, Lynn, and Margery should come over today."

"Text me Erin's number, if you don't mind."

Cassie got nervous for a moment. What if Erin was mean to Mary Ellen? Although Cassie was pretty sure Mary Ellen could hold her own against Texas.

"I will," she replied. "Thank you so much," she added.

"Everything will be fine, you know," Mary Ellen said. "They're just being silly."

Cassie wasn't sure if it was the steadiness of Mary Ellen's voice, but for the first time since yesterday she felt like things might be okay.

CHAPTER 11
Everything That Really Counts

When the doorbell rang later that afternoon, Cassie's palms began to sweat. First, she didn't even know who it would be. She hadn't heard a thing from anyone. She kept telling herself that it had to all work out. She had faith in Texas, Maine, and Mary Ellen. But so much could still go wrong.

Cassie ran down the steps and opened the door. It was Erin and Laura. They had a wheelie suitcase with them. She noticed they looked a little sheepish, which made Cassie feel better.

"Hi!" they both exclaimed as they walked in.

"Are you moving in or what?" Cassie asked, relieved at how casual they were.

"Outfit breakdowns. Seriously. We have no idea what to wear tonight," Erin said.

Cassie led them to the kitchen, where Sheila greeted them with fresh lemonade and hugs.

The doorbell chimed again. Cassie ran to get it. Her mind was reeling. How had Mary Ellen done this?

She opened the door to find Etoile on the stoop, wearing bell-bottom jeans and a fuchsia peasant blouse. She was flanked by Mary Ellen, Lynn, and Margery.

"Wow! Hi, everyone!" Cassie said, opening the screen door.

She gave Etoile a quick hug. She'd never seen her so bright. "Hi, megawatts!" she said. She thought it best, for now, to just pretend like nothing had happened last night.

Etoile didn't return Cassie's hug, but she didn't step away either. She, too, seemed a little sheepish. "I just thought I should brighten things up a bit today," she replied softly. "I still have no clue what to wear tonight," she added.

Cassie didn't care what Etoile wore tonight— she was just glad her BFF was coming to her party!

Etoile hauled a big backpack from the step behind her and went to set it down in the living room. Meanwhile, Lynn, Margery, and Mary Ellen turned their focus to Cassie.

"Cass!" Lynn shouted.

"It's your big day!" Margery said.

Cassie gave both girls a big hug, thrilled to see them.

"Looking good, Mary Ellen!" Cassie said. She was sure Mary Ellen didn't realize it but she was wearing a very mod outfit. Dark, dark jeans; a black, fitted tee with red stripes across it; and red flats.

"Thanks. It's just a T-shirt and—"

Cassie cut her off immediately. "Just say 'thank you.'"

Mary Ellen laughed. "Thank you. Are you doing okay?" she asked, lowering her voice.

"I'm better now that you're here," she whispered.

Mary Ellen smiled. "Good. It's going to be fine." She looped her arm through Cassie's. "Just let things go for right now. They're all going to figure it out on their own."

"I don't know," Cassie said. "Are you sure? How did you convince them to come?" She watched out of the corner of her eye as Etoile made her way from the living room to the kitchen.

"I called both parties and told them to get it together and to get to your house. I told them that they would never want to be remembered as the ones who ruined your thirteenth birthday," Mary Ellen said very seriously, as if she were reading from a book report.

"And?" Cassie whispered.

"Erin hung up on me."

"No! I am so sorry!" Cassie said.

"It was fine. I called her back three times before she answered. Then she was okay."

"And Etoile?" Cassie asked.

"She's pretty upset. She wouldn't tell me why exactly but I think you need to talk to her."

"I do. I made a stupid, big mistake," Cassie said sadly.

"But there's one detail I'm leaving out," Mary Ellen said.

"What?"

"Erin and Laura don't know that Etoile is going to be here," Mary Ellen said nervously.

"What?!" Cassie gasped.

"And vice versa," Mary Ellen added.

"Oh no."

"Oh yes. I couldn't convince them otherwise, so I kind of fibbed."

Mary Ellen and Cassie looked toward the kitchen, worried. Cassie tightly grasped Mary Ellen's arm and they slowly crept in that direction.

Etoile was standing by the counter, drinking lemonade with Sheila. Erin and Laura were at the table, munching on the cutest, tiniest cucumber sandwiches that Sheila set out for them.

There was an awkward feeling in the air, but it was civil. Nobody was fighting or being mean. That was enough for Cassie to let go of Mary Ellen's arm.

Sheila locked eyes with Cassie and smiled. *"Nice work,"* she mouthed happily.

Cassie smiled. And took a deep breath.

"All right, ladies," Sheila said. "You have exactly two hours before we have to head to the party."

"Two hours?!" both Erin and Etoile shrieked. They looked at each other and smiled slightly.

"That is definitely not enough time!" Erin said.

"We have to get moving!" Etoile chimed in.

Mary Ellen spoke up then. "Okay, before you all start running around getting ready, I would like to make a toast." She poured herself a cup of lemonade, then raised it. "To Cassie. On the day after her thirteenth birthday." She paused.

Cassie glanced nervously around the kitchen. Her eyes landed on Sheila, who was smiling widely. Sheila's smile always comforted Cassie.

"When Cassie first came to Oak Grove, I thought she'd never last. And I wanted to make sure of that. I was as mean as could be," Mary Ellen said.

Etoile looked at Cassie with sad eyes.

"So we've heard," Erin said.

"Very funny," Mary Ellen said, giving it right back to Erin. "Seriously, though. Cassie dressed like she was going to a fashion show. She wore lip gloss and tons of makeup. She had this twangy accent. It was like she was an alien!"

"Hey, watch it there, darlin', she learned her makeup tips from me," Sheila said jokingly.

Everyone laughed.

Mary Ellen continued. "Then, she started to do all of this great stuff. She's doing *almost* as well as me in school, which drives me crazy!"

More laughter.

"She's totally funny. She does a great job on Yearbook. And she is loved by everyone who meets her. Really, it's sickening. There couldn't be two people at Oak Grove . . . in Maine . . . on the planet . . . more different than Cassie and me. We don't dress the same. We don't talk the same. But somehow, she has found a way to get past how unkind I was to her when we first met. And to become my friend."

Cassie's eyes filled with tears.

"And I think she's realized that I'm not so bad either. Even though I don't condition my hair three times a day."

"Three times a week!" Cassie shouted. "You don't want it to get too soft!" She giggled.

All the girls chuckled.

"So," Mary Ellen continued, practically glowing in the afternoon sun, "I want to wish you a happy birthday, Cassie. You are one of the best people I've ever been lucky enough to meet." Mary Ellen raised her glass high.

Cassie looked around the room. Etoile's eyes were wet; Erin's and Laura's were the same.

"Happy birthday, Cassie," Mary Ellen said. With that all the girls raised their glasses and said, "Happy birthday!"

Cassie couldn't believe the response from the girls.

"Before you guys get ready, I'd like to propose a little bit of a game," Mary Ellen said.

"What kind of game?" Laura asked.

"So, you guys know the show *Wicked*, right?" Mary Ellen asked.

Cassie still couldn't believe Mary Ellen was a *Wicked* fan.

"Well, I say we follow the rules of *Wicked*. Elphaba, the green witch, had no idea what it was like to be blond and popular. And Glinda, the popular one, had no idea what it was like to be green and unpopular. But they taught each other to see the other side."

"Okay . . ." Etoile said, unsure of where Mary Ellen was going.

"So, I say the girls from Texas get to dress the girls from Maine any way they please."

Erin and Laura smiled. "Woo-hoo! I'd love to get my hands on you guys!" Erin said.

"AND," Mary Ellen said. "The Maine girls get to dress the Texas girls."

Erin and Laura stopped smiling then.

"Love it!" Lynn said. "I'm in!"

Mary Ellen looked across the kitchen counter at Erin and Laura. "And you?"

"I'm only in if we're allowed to dress you, too," Erin said.

"Me?" Mary Ellen asked. "I don't do stuff like that."

"Then we're out. Sorry," Laura said.

Margery laughed. "You gotta do it, Mary Ellen."

Mary Ellen looked at Cassie. Took a deep breath. "Fine. For Cassie."

"Woo-hoo!" Laura shouted. Everyone in the kitchen laughed and headed up to Cassie's room. Cassie let out a breath of relief. She couldn't believe Mary Ellen's crazy idea was working!

Within ten minutes, Cassie's room looked like backstage at a fashion show. There were dresses and skirts and shirts and shoes everywhere.

They decided to start by dressing the Maine girls first. From the bounty of clothes and accessories on Cassie's bed, the Texas girls began picking and choosing what looks worked for which girl.

Margery and Lynn were easy. They were up for anything and wound up in fringed, suede skirts: Margery's maroon and Lynn's chocolate. Margery chose Laura's bejeweled denim jacket and a cool striped tee for underneath. Lynn looked perfect in a blue gingham shirt, and even borrowed a red bandanna from Cassie to tie around her neck— completing the cutest cowgirl look!

Etoile seemed nervous as she watched the makeovers. She lingered in the corner, biting her manicured nails. Erin and Laura applied thick makeup to Lynn's and Margery's faces and teased their hair to ferocious heights, all four of them laughing the whole way through. Cassie hoped that after all the drama, Erin and Laura would be as kind and gentle with Etoile.

"Lynn and Margery, why don't you help Mary Ellen look through the other stuff we brought?" Erin said, adding a final touch of sculpting spray to Lynn's hair. Mary Ellen went pale, but followed the two girls to Cassie's bed to decide on an outfit.

To Cassie's surprise, Laura walked right over to Etoile. She didn't say anything, but she took Etoile by the hand and sat her down at Cassie's desk.

"Now, what colors do you love?" Laura asked. "And no beige or navy. I'm talking COLOR, missy," Laura said.

Etoile cracked a smile. "I do like purple."

Whew, Cassie thought.

"Really?" Erin called from across the room. "Now *that's* a color!" Erin ducked down and dug through her suitcase. "How about this?" She pulled out a gorgeous purple dress that had real shimmer to it. The sleeves were slightly too poufy for Etoile, Cassie was certain.

"That's a good one!" Etoile said. She jumped up and walked over to Erin.

"Try it. It's one of my favorites," Erin said sweetly.

"Are you sure?" Etoile asked.

"Right now, I'm sure of two things," Erin replied. "The first is that you are going to look perfect in this dress. And the next is . . ." Erin paused and shook her head, her cheeks turning pink. "The next is that I haven't been the nicest person to you."

Cassie gasped, but it was a hopeful gasp.

Laura, seeing what was going on, walked over to join Erin and Etoile. "Neither have I," she said softly.

"We are so sorry for saying those mean things yesterday," Erin continued, and Laura nodded. "It's not who we are at all. I know that might be hard to believe, but it's true."

Etoile swallowed and spoke quietly. "I wasn't the nicest person either," she said. "I mean, I told you to spit your gum out! I can't believe I did that."

Cassie quickly hurried over and joined the girls. "No, *I* told you to spit your gum out. I shouldn't have done that," she said. "I guess we've all been acting badly."

Etoile nodded. "I didn't think it would be so hard, bringing two different groups of friends together," she said thoughtfully.

"Cass, when you moved away, we were devastated," Erin said, looking at Cassie with tears in her eyes. "We never wanted you to know, though, because you didn't need that on top of all the other stress you had to deal with. And when we heard that some of the people in Maine were being mean to you, and that you weren't totally fitting in, we, well . . ."

"We were sort of happy," Laura confessed.

Cassie was shocked. *How could that be?* she thought, glancing from Erin to Laura in confusion.

"Not because you were upset and going through a hard time!" Laura clarified quickly. "But we thought you'd maybe move back to Houston and be with us again."

Cassie choked up. There was a time when she'd *wanted* to move back to Houston. But things had changed.

Erin stepped closer to Etoile. "And then Cassie met you and she was happy again. And sounded like herself again. So I guess we got a little jealous. Or something."

"Maybe more than a little jealous," Laura whispered with a shy shrug.

"But I was jealous of you, too!" Etoile cried, putting her hand on Erin's arm. "I mean, you guys have so much history between you."

"It's true that we do, but we didn't mean to

make you feel left out," Erin said. "We were being snobby and silly."

"And when we heard Mary Ellen's speech in the kitchen," Laura said, glancing at Erin, "I think we both realized that we actually *are* glad that you're settled here, Cass. If we couldn't be happy for you, then we wouldn't be true friends."

"You guys!" Cassie said, tearing up.

Erin nodded, giving Etoile's hand a squeeze. "And we're happy that she's met you, Etoile. If it can't be us who make her laugh every day, we're glad it's you."

"Wow," Etoile said. "Thank you."

"Will you forgive us?" Erin asked Etoile.

"Only if you forgive me, too!" Etoile said, grinning.

"And will you forgive us, Cass?" Laura added. "We're so sorry we ruined your birthday."

"Of course I forgive you!" Cassie said. "And my birthday's not over yet!"

All four girls burst out laughing, and Cassie felt her heart lift with relief. She opened her arms, and all four of them piled into a big cuddle puddle.

"Thank goodness!" Cassie exclaimed. "I thought y'all would *never* make up!"

"And now that we have," Laura said, handing the purple dress to Etoile, "get this dress on and knock us out!"

"Cass, can you help me?" Etoile asked as she took the dress and held it against herself. "I'll need you to do the zipper in the back."

"Sure," Cassie said. Together, they walked to the spare bedroom across the hall. Cassie was glad to have a moment alone with Etoile.

"I know Erin and Laura apologized to you, but I am so sorry about everything, too," Cassie said. "I should have tried harder to make you feel more a part of the group."

"No, it's fine," Etoile said. "*You* were great. I was being a jealous jerk."

Cassie sat down on the daybed. "But I should have told you about Jonah," she said softly.

Etoile nodded. "I *was* upset about that. I hope you know you can tell me anything."

"Of course I know that!" Cassie said. "I guess I felt mixed up about Jonah myself. I think maybe we have crushes on each other. But that's it."

"I wondered a little bit about that. You two are always talking. And I think it's so great!" Etoile said.

"You do?" Cassie asked, surprised.

"Of course!" Etoile said.

"But you hate him!" Cassie said, laughing.

"I hate him like he's my brother. But I love him. And I love you! So it's sort of perfect!"

Cassie gave Etoile a big hug. "He gave me a birthday present, actually."

"Really? What is it?" Etoile asked.

Cassie popped up and ran across the hall to get the headband.

"Ready?" she asked, walking back into the spare bedroom with the headband behind her back.

"Oh no. Ready," Etoile said.

Cassie pulled it out from behind her back, and Etoile started laughing immediately. "It's hideous!" she said.

"I know! I know! But so sweet!" Cassie said.

"Okay, listen, if I had known, I would have made sure he bought you something better!"

They hugged again. "Thank you for understanding," Cassie said.

"That's what friends are for," Etoile said, and she and Cassie exchanged a warm smile.

"Okay, we better get back in there," Cassie

said, finally zipping Etoile into the purple dress. "Mary Ellen is up next and she looks like a deer in headlights."

When Cassie and Etoile returned to Cassie's bedroom, Etoile looking stunning in her new dress, they were shocked to see Erin and Laura in their new Maine outfits.

Erin looked like a natural in a khaki shirt dress with a navy-blue sash belt. And Laura was radiant in a pair of gray skinny jeans and a maroon and white striped button-down, cinched by a skinny belt. Erin wore Lynn's little navy-blue bow earrings, and Laura wore Margery's gold stud earrings. Both girls had their hair down in soft waves, and only wore lip gloss.

"Wow!" Cassie said, barely recognizing her friends. "You guys look incredible!"

"I know, it's weird, but I'm kind of liking the understated look," Erin said, studying herself in the mirror.

"Are you sure my hair doesn't look too flat?" Laura asked, frowning, which made Cassie giggle. Laura's hair looked luscious and just right.

When Erin and Laura turned their attention to Etoile, they screamed. "You go, girl!" they shouted.

"Get into the hair and makeup chair and we will spray you up!" Laura said.

"I'm ready!" Etoile laughed.

To Cassie's delight and surprise, Etoile actually looked great with her hair big. Erin did Etoile's makeup, which included the slightest hint of cat eyes. The effect was very mod-retro, and Etoile clearly loved it.

Next up was Mary Ellen.

The poor girl cowered in the corner. Cassie went over to her and said firmly, "You have no choice or say in any of these matters. I need you to cooperate, McGinty. Can you do that?"

Mary Ellen nodded, looking shocked.

"This is what we picked out with Lynn and Margery," Laura said. She held up her own pair of Seven jeans, a fringy vest, and Cassie's favorite pair of red cowboy boots.

"LOVE it!" Cassie said.

"Okay, I can be a good sport. Let's get this done," Mary Ellen said, ever the taskmaster.

"All right!" Laura cheered, turning the music up.

And before Cassie knew it, the music took over and Mary Ellen was reveling in her transformation. She examined herself in the mirror, admiring the jeans, the vest, and the very pair of cowboy boots she had once mocked. She even asked for hair-sprayed hair and cat eyes, just like Etoile!

After her hair and makeup were complete, she smiled at herself in the mirror. "Look at me!" Mary Ellen said giddily.

"Girl," Laura said, "you are C-U-T-E! Cute!"

Everyone squealed, and clamored for pictures. Cassie took shot after shot of the girls with her digital camera.

"Cassie, can you take a picture with my phone?" Mary Ellen asked.

"Of course! Why?" Cassie asked as she took Mary Ellen's phone from her.

"I want my mom to see!" she said.

That made Cassie so happy. Mrs. McGinty rocked some serious style and Cassie knew she'd love seeing Mary Ellen all decked out.

"And, now, for the birthday girl . . ." Etoile said, turning to Cassie. "What will it be?"

"That's easy," Cassie said. All week long she'd agonized over what to wear on her big night, and now, after all the ups and downs with her Texas and Maine friends, she finally knew. She walked to her closet and reached into the back. She pulled out her teal Nicky Hilton dress, the one she wore on the first day of school at Oak Grove.

"Yes!" Etoile cried. "That's the one!"

Cassie smiled as she held the dress against herself. She'd certainly changed a lot since that first day at Oak Grove, but it was nice to remember her old self sometimes.

The other girls agreed and before Cassie knew it, she was in the dress, Lynn and Margery were setting her hair in curlers, and Erin and Laura were doing her makeup.

When she was done and gorgeous, Etoile walked over to Cassie, holding Jonah's headband. In no time at all, Etoile had unbraided it and retied it so it was a very cool fabric necklace, which she then put around Cassie's neck.

"What do you think?" Etoile asked.

"I love it! Thank you so much!"

Lynn pulled out her camera and started snapping away. Cassie was thrilled. Posing, laughing, and primping—three of Cassie's favorite things— were happening with Cassie's favorite people.

Sheila stuck her head into Cassie's room. "Look at you guys!" she said happily. "You're all too fabulous!"

"Thanks!" the girls chorused, spinning around in their new outfits.

Sheila grinned. "All right, fashion plates," she said, "get your skates and let's go have some fun!"

As the girls filed out of her room, Cassie took one last look at herself in the mirror. Something was missing. She turned to her bed and saw Etoile's green feather hair clip and slid it into her hair. It was the perfect addition.

CHAPTER 12

Sparks!

The Sparks Roller Rink looked even prettier than Cassie remembered. Big glass doors led into a very cool, sort of futuristic lobby, with neon pink stripes everywhere and a smooth gray granite counter for skate rentals. This was 1980s chic at its finest!

The three original Texas girls had their own matching skates. Cassie, Erin, and Laura had been skate queens back in Houston. Cassie supposed Erin and Laura still were skate queens, even without her!

"We're going to head to the rentals counter," Etoile said, her big hair bobbing above her as she spoke. Cassie grinned. Now that all the drama was out of the way, she loved seeing Etoile all done up like a Texas girl!

"Okay, we're going to wait on the benches," Cassie said, pointing. She scanned the room to make sure no one had arrived early for the party. Etoile nodded and led the other girls to the rentals counter.

The Texas three walked to the benches. Cassie plunked down in the middle and they began lacing up their skates. Seeing the three pairs next to one another sent a chill of happiness through Cassie. It had been way too long since they'd done this together.

"Thank you so much for coming," Cassie said. She put her arms around Erin and Laura.

"Thank you for having us," Laura said.

"Thank you for *dealing* with us," Erin said, laughing.

"It's okay," Cassie said quietly. "It was great of you to apologize to Etoile. I know it's hard, adjusting to the new . . . well, me. I feel like it's hard for me to juggle my two lives."

"But you're doing a beautiful job," Erin said, giving Cassie a quick hug.

"So, since we have a moment alone, we wanted

133

to give you your gift now, if that's okay," Laura piped up.

"You didn't have to get me a thing! You're here! That's your gift!" Cassie said sincerely.

"Oh, please!" Erin laughed. "A thirteenth birthday calls for a full-on gift." She pulled out a plain cardboard box and a small card.

"We didn't wrap it because it's not green to waste paper like that," Laura said.

Cassie smiled. "That's so awesome. Thank you."

Cassie opened the card first, of course. The message inside was simple and perfect.

We'll always be together.
Love love, Erin and Laura

She opened the box to find a charm in the shape of Maine. Cassie gasped.

"The reason we knew about the charm bracelet," Erin explained, "was because we called Sheila to ask what to get you. We wanted to make sure we gave you something that you would love here in Maine."

"You guys did not have to do this," Cassie said, touched.

"Yes, we did," Erin said. "You have Texas in your heart . . ."

"And now Maine in your hand," Laura finished.

Cassie was blinking away tears when she heard a boy's voice. "Uh, is this a private party or can anyone come?"

She knew it was Jonah. She looked up to find him standing with Seth. "Hi!" she said brightly, quickly wiping her eyes.

Jonah and Seth both looked very cute. Jonah was wearing dark blue jeans and a light blue shirt, with a skinny little tie.

"Wow!" Cassie said. "You look awesome!" She immediacy regretted saying those words. Did she sound like a dork?

Erin gave Cassie a nudge.

"Oh, guys, these are my friends from Texas," Cassie said quickly. "Erin and Laura. Guys, this is Seth and . . . Jonah."

As she said "Jonah" she lightly pinched the girls on their arms.

"It's so nice to meet y'all!" Laura said, standing,

almost tripping over her skates. She shook the boys' hands.

Then Erin stood. "It is a pleasure to meet you guys. Cassie's told us a lot about you."

Seth and Jonah took turns shaking Erin's hand.

Cassie could just tell Erin and Laura were sizing up Jonah, and that her friends were bursting to talk to her about him.

Feeling awkward, Cassie said, "Seth, Etoile and the others are over at rentals."

"Okay, thanks. I got my own," he said, pointing down to a rad pair of graffitied skates.

"Those are awesome!" Cassie said.

"Um, what about these?" Jonah said, pointing down to his own gray pinstriped pair.

"Wow, very chic!" Erin said.

"I'll go get the other girls," Seth said.

"Want to come with us?" Jonah asked, putting his hand out for Cassie.

"Oh," Cassie's heart raced. "Um, I should wait here for . . ."

"Sure she does!" Erin said, practically knocking Cassie off of the bench. "We'll be right behind you!"

Erin is going to pay for this, Cassie thought.

She tightened the lace on her skate and quickly pulled it into a bow. She reached her hand up and Jonah took it. He smiled.

"Happy birthday, Knight. This party is gonna be awesome."

She clasped tightly to his hand and led him across the room. *It already is,* she thought.

A while later, all of Cassie's guests had arrived. They were assembled in the snack bar, underneath a HAPPY BIRTHDAY, CASSIE sign that Sheila had ordered for the party. Perfection. Everyone was snapping pictures and updating their Facebook pages. Cassie totally felt like a young star with the paparazzi. She loved that feeling!

"Okay, everyone," the DJ said over the loudspeaker. "We have Cassie Knight in the house, celebrating her thirteenth birthday."

Everyone in Cassie's party applauded and hooted.

"So, let's get you out there on the floor, Cassie!" the DJ shouted.

Cassie grabbed Etoile, Erin, and Laura. "Let's go!" she cried.

They all skated together onto the floor. Laura rolled up and grabbed Etoile's hand and the foursome skated, the lights twinkling around them, the music from the speakers clean and clear. Soon, Margery, Lynn, and Mary Ellen joined them.

Erin and Etoile split off together. Cassie and Laura grasped hands and laughed at how funny the two looked skating up ahead of them. Erin's hair was straight and simple, with a navy ribbon through it. And Etoile's was higher than the Leaning Tower of Pisa!

"Can you believe how different we all look?" Laura asked over the music.

"It's so amazing!" Cassie said. "Because even though we're dressed differently than we usually are, we all still look like ourselves. I love that about us. And I love us. All of us!"

Laura squeezed Cassie's hand tight. "Well, we do sort of look the same. Except maybe for one person," Laura said, pointing.

Cassie turned her head and saw Mary Ellen leaning against the wall, hair teased and sprayed to the ceiling, wearing Laura's jeans and the fringy vest, absentmindedly chomping on gum, which she never did in real life.

"I think that might be the best birthday gift I'll ever get!" Cassie said.

"Seriously, she looks like she's right at home," Laura said.

The song came to an end. Etoile swooped over. "You have one sec?" she asked Cassie.

"Of course!"

Etoile led Cassie over to a table away from everyone. "I wanted to give you your gift last night. And then I felt so stupid and bad and just—"

"Don't even worry about it," Cassie said, meaning it. It was all in the past.

"So, anyway, I wanted to give you this," Etoile said, handing her a large unwrapped box. Cassie expected no wrapping paper from Etoile, of course.

Rather than attach a card, she'd written her message on the box with a Sharpie.

For the best friend I've ever had. The best friend that I never thought I would have. On her thirteenth birthday.
Hearts and stuff, Etoile

Cassie tore open the box. In it, she found an envelope with four tickets to *Wicked*.

For tomorrow night.

"I can't believe this!" Cassie said.

"I'd originally gotten just two tickets for us, but I called the theater today and they were able to change the reservation. We'll all go now—you, me, Erin, and Laura," Etoile announced, all big-eyed and beaming.

"This is the best present ever!" Cassie squealed. "We're going to have so much fun!"

"I know!" Etoile said.

"Do Erin and Laura know?"

"Not yet!"

"I can't wait to tell them!" Cassie gave Etoile a big hug.

Just then Jonah and Seth skated up. "Mind if I interrupt?" Jonah asked Etoile.

"Not at all!" she said. She let go of Cassie's hand and took Seth's. As they skated away, Etoile looked back for a moment, popping her eyes at Cassie, who smiled back at her.

Jonah took Cassie's hand, gingerly at first, and just as a slow song came on, led her back to the main area of the rink.

The two skated together, not talking much. Cassie spent the first moments worrying about what she looked like, if her hand was sweating, what would happen if she fell. But then she had a realization. This was Jonah that she was skating with. He'd been her friend from the first moments at Oak Grove. She didn't have to worry about that stuff. They were friends first.

She grabbed his hand a bit tighter. "Follow me," she said.

Before he could even answer, Cassie led Jonah into the center of the wooden rink. She turned to him and grabbed him like they were dancing together. She figured he knew how to skate, since he had his own pair of skates—and she was right! Before she knew it, they were skating backward, and even did a few spins together. She heard Etoile and the girls cheering them from the sidelines.

The song ended then and they even did a slight dip. Cassie felt energized and giddy.

"Cassie Knight," the DJ said, "please head back to your party area."

"Cake time?" Jonah asked.

"Um, that's supposed to be a surprise," she said, nudging him.

"Oh, c'mon. A surprise? You're having a birthday party. You get a cake," he said.

She appreciated his sense of humor. "Oh, come on!" she said, pushing off and grabbing his hand.

When they got to the tables, everyone was gathered around. Sheila and Paul stood in the back, taking pictures like mad.

Etoile, Erin, and Laura slowly brought a huge cake out from the back, covered in beautiful, delicate flowers, complete with thirteen candles on it. Mary Ellen skated to the center of the group.

"Everyone!" she called. "Sing with me!"

They all began to sing "Happy Birthday" to Cassie.

She stood there, beaming, camera flashes going off all around her. There were so many big smiles twinkling at her, so many people singing to her, celebrating her.

There was Texas. There was Maine. Sheila and Paul. Seth and Jonah. Mary Ellen and her gum.

Cassie Cyan Knight was thirteen.

She lived in Maine.

And the two worlds that she loved were finally becoming one. She'd gotten her wish from the night before.

So, what could she possibly wish for today?

As the singing ended, it came to her. The group clapped and cheered. She took a big, deep breath and leaned over, careful to steady herself on the table for fear that her skates would catch her dress and send her tumbling.

Her big, shiny wish floated in her head.

She focused on it and exhaled.

The candles flickered, jumped, and then were out. Cassie opened her eyes to smiles and applause.

She couldn't wait until her next wish came true.

Take a sneak peek at

Petal Pushers

An irresistible new series about
four sisters and one hectic
flower store . . .

I stepped forward and opened the door. "Welcome to Flowers on Fairfield," I said in my most professional-sounding voice. "Can I help you?"

The woman looked to be in her midtwenties. Her long, blonde hair was pulled into a perfect ponytail, not a strand out of place. She had big, blue eyes and was wearing light pink lipstick. She was just so pretty and perfect looking, like a mannequin.

Oddly enough, she had her hands in the air, as if she was afraid to touch anything. *Maybe she's one of those germ-phobic weirdos,* I thought.

"I just got a mani-pedi!" she exclaimed as she stepped inside. "Don't want to smudge my nails!" She smiled, flashing her straight, white teeth. I found myself nodding in sympathy and returning her grin, although I wasn't totally sure what she was talking about. Manny who?

"Oh, okay," I said.

"Would you be a sweetheart and put Louis on the floor?" she asked me.

"Louis?" I asked.

She looked at me like I had two heads. "Louis Vuitton?" she said, nodding toward the bag slung over her shoulder. That's when I noticed that there was a tiny, shivering dog poking its face out of her large purse. I reached inside and picked up the dog. As I placed the pet on the floor, I blinked. Was Louis wearing a tiny, black leather motorcycle jacket? Why, yes he was.

The customer looked around. "So this is it," she said with a sigh. "I was hoping it would be . . . fancier."

My mouth fell open. How rude! Luckily, Gran sensed my annoyance and stepped right in, putting on her most gracious smile. "How can we help you, dear?" she said.

"My name is Olivia Post," the woman said. She held out her left hand. A huge diamond sparkled on her ring finger. "I got engaged last night!" she gushed. "Five carats, cushion cut, can you believe it?"

We all oohed and ahhed although I don't know if any of us knew exactly what "cushion cut" meant. "So," Olivia continued. "I wanted to have a spring wedding. May nineteenth!"

Gran smiled, but she looked distracted. I knew she was calculating how many weeks that would give us. Her widened eyes said it all — not many.

"Will it be a large wedding?" Gramps wanted to know.

"Oh, only a couple hundred guests," explained Olivia.

Gramps and I exchanged glances. That was huge by anyone's standards!

"But I really want it to have an intimate feel," Olivia continued. "And it's got to be special. I'm thinking ice sculptures, a couple of chocolate fountains, a sushi station. . . . So the flowers, of course, have to be exquisite," she concluded.

Gran looked panicked. In two weeks she and Gramps were going to be snorkeling with the sea turtles. *Would* my mom be able to handle this? Slowly, Gran shook her head. "I don't know if this is a good time," she said. "You see, there's going to be a change in management . . ."

I cleared my throat. "There's no problem at all,"

I heard myself saying. *Wait! Stop!* my brain protested. But my mouth kept moving. "We will give you the wedding of your dreams. The most exquisite floral arrangements this town has ever seen!"

Everyone stared at me in shock. Except Olivia. She just smiled at me as if twelve-year-olds routinely took charge of planning weddings. "Excellent!" she said. Checking her nails, she picked up Louis Vuitton. Then she whipped out her cell phone and placed a call.

"Hello. I am interested in ordering six dozen white doves, spray painted pink," she said on her way out.

The door shut behind her. "Oh, Del, you were great!" cried Gran, giving me a squeeze. Then she looked into my eyes. "Do you really think you can handle it?"

"No problem, Gran," I said. My heart was pounding. I could hardly believe it. I had just agreed to do the flowers for an impossible-to-please Bridezilla with unrealistic expectations. In a matter of weeks, no less.

My stomach sank. What had I gotten myself into?

Read all about Cassie Knight: Miss Popularity!

Bubbly, popular Cassie moves from Texas to cold, snowy Maine. But the students at her new school don't appreciate her fabulous personality! Will Cassie be friendless forever?

Cassie's class is going on a camping trip! But this fashionista is not quite prepared for hiking and white-water rafting. Can Cassie make it through the trip in style?

Candy Apple books . . . just for you.
Sweet. Fresh. Fun. Take a bite!

candy apple

Read them all!

Life, Starring Me!

Callie for President

Drama Queen

I've Got a Secret

Confessions of a Bitter Secret Santa

Super Sweet 13

The Boy Next Door

The Sister Switch

Snowfall Surprise

Rumor Has It

The Sweetheart Deal

The Accidental Cheerleader

The Babysitting Wars

Star-Crossed

Accidentally
Fabulous

Accidentally
Famous

Accidentally
Fooled

Accidentally
Friends

How to Be a Girly Girl in
Just Ten Days

Ice Dreams

Juicy Gossip

Making Waves

Miss Popularity

Miss Popularity
Goes Camping

Miss Popularity
and the Best Friend Disaster

Totally Crushed

Wish You Were Here,
Liza

See You Soon,
Samantha

Miss You, Mina

Winner Takes All

POISON APPLE BOOKS

The Dead End

This Totally Bites!

Miss Fortune

Now You See Me...

Midnight Howl

Her Evil Twin

THRILLING. BONE-CHILLING.
THESE BOOKS HAVE BITE!